W9-CZW-358

Still Caught Up With A Trap God

Carmen & Raul A Hood Love

By Shaniya Dennis

Copyright © 2020 Shaniya Dennis
Published by Kellz K Publishing
All rights reserved. No part of this book may be
reproduced, distributed, or transmitted in any form or by
any means, including photocopying, recording, or other
electronic or mechanical methods without prior written
consent of the publisher, except in brief quotations
embodied in critical reviews and certain other
noncommercial uses permitted by copyright law. For
permission requests, please contact:
kellzkpublishing@gmail.com
This is a work of fiction. Names, characters, places, and
incidents either are the products of the author's imagination
or are used fictitiously. Any references or similarities to
actual events, real people, living or dead, or to the real
locals are intended to give the novel a sense of reality. Any
similarity in other names, characters, places, and incidents
are entirely coincidental. The publisher does not have any
control and does not assume any responsibility for author
or third-party websites or their content.
The unauthorized reproduction or distribution of
this copyrighted works is punishable by law. No part of the
e-book may be scanned, uploaded to, or downloaded from
file sharing sites, or distributed in any other way via the
Internet or any other means, electronic or print, without the
publisher's permission. Criminal copyright infringement,
including infringement without monetary gain, is
investigated by the FBI and is punishable by up to five
years in federal prison and a fine of $250,000
(www.fbi.gov/ipr/).

Acknowledgements:

I would like to acknowledge my supporters it's been a minute since I put out a book and you guys still have been rocking with me. I appreciate you all.

This book is dedicated to my brother Duke. I miss you and love you so much. You know the vibes legends don't ever die. I'll see you at the crossroads.

Where we left off in Caught Up with A Trap God…

Raven stood in the mirror looking at herself. Today was the day she would become one with the man she'd been loving for most of her life. Her two kids, Jr, and Rayna, were being held by the babysitter they hired shortly after Rayna was born. Hearing someone knock on the door, Raven looked, not knowing who waited on the other side. She didn't have friends, not one since she and Niomi fell out over the bank situation a little over a year ago. She had no family, and she knew it wasn't Diggy. So, whoever was knocking was beyond her. Going to the door. she cracked it and got a surprise of her life when she saw Niomi standing there in a royal blue bridesmaid dress.

"How did you know?" Raven asked, tears in her eyes as she moved to the side and let her best friend in.

"Diggy told Renz and he told me. I couldn't let my bestie get married without being there. I can't lie, I was so mad at you for not telling me and leaving me in the dark. I forgave Renz and I forgive you too. Look at these babies, they are so cute."

"Yes, my Jr and my princess."

"So how are things with his moms?"

"Bitch, she done had him and got ghost. Diggy came to the hospital to visit them and said he would be back the next day. Her ass dipped and left Jr in there. Weeks later, she was found dead. I'm happy too. Diggy told me that bitch put a date rape drug in his cup when he came to put up Jr.'s bed. The bitch better be lucky someone got to her before I could. Now I'm a mommy of two kids who are only months apart."

Raven and Niomi both looked on at the kids smiling. When Diggy called Raven over the phone and told her that he was bringing Jr home to live with them, she didn't know how to feel about it. It was one thing to know that your fiancé stepped out and conceived a child on you. It was another thing for that child to be under your roof, reminding you every day of the man you love infidelities. Raven wasn't too happy to hear that. Not wanting to voice her opinions to Diggy, she just simply concurred to it. The moment her eyes landed on Jr., Raven fell in love with him. There was no way she couldn't love him like he came out of her. He looked just like his father while Rayna, on the other hand, looked just like Raven.

"Wow," Niomi said and Raven nodded her head. They talked and caught up for a minute before another knock was on the door. This time it was Jaliyah telling Niomi to put on a dress. Niomi was so confused.

"Don't ask questions just put it on."

Once Niomi got dressed, someone came to do her hair and makeup.

"What's going on?" Niomi asked, not understanding.

Raven giggled because Renz texted her to make sure it was cool with her. Of course, Raven was happy. Renz proposed to Niomi last month and she said yes. Renz, not wanting to wait any longer to get married, decided they could have a wedding with Diggy and Raven now, and then have another one that she could plan. Everyone was in on it except Niomi, she had no idea.

An hour later, her makeup and hair was done and she was dressed. Raven and Nicole walked side by side down the aisle. When Niomi realized what was going on, tears came down her face as she noticed Renz next to Diggy at the altar. Raul was behind them in a silver suit while Carmen and Jaliyah, the bridesmaids, wore royal blue dresses same colored dress Niomi originally wore. Both men stared at the women who had their heart, feeling emotional. This moment would seal their fate. This very moment was the moment they had been waiting for. No more trapping, robbing banks, or illegal businesses; they both had successful companies. Diggy with his car lots around the city and Renz with his temp agency, now they both were about to marry the woman they loved. Renz and Diggy both shared a brotherly look. Although their mouths didn't speak it, their eyes did. Silently, they were congratulating each other on the move they were making. Raven walked in front of Diggy while Niomi stood in front of Renz. The pastor got the process rolling and within twenty minutes, they were all married.

***

Niomi and Raven sat at the balcony to Raven's penthouse suite. Diggy and Renz were in the room smoking. The wind blew, giving them both a cold chill.

"Can you believe we are married women now?"

"I mean I can believe I am. I knew I'd be Diggy's wife one day. You, on the other hand, would have never expected it. You were a virgin who didn't want anything to do with men, now you're married and in love with a thug."

"Plus pregnant." Niomi beamed and Raven shouted. "Girl, why are you yelling? Be quiet before for the guys come out and think something's wrong. I haven't told Renz yet, I just found out earlier today." The words had just left Niomi's mouth when Diggy and Renz both rushed onto the balcony.

"What's wrong?" Renz rushed to Niomi's side while Diggy ran to Raven's.

Niomi rolled her eyes as Raven giggled. "I'm pregnant," she told Renz and he smiled.

"I knew that pussy was feeling different."

"You're happy, right?"

"Hell yea! You my wife, why wouldn't I be? I'ma put so many kids inside of you."

"That's so nasty, but cute. Let's make a toast."

"I can't drink."

"So, bitch? Act like you got a cup in your hand, hold it up and make a toast."

"To what?"

"To being caught up with fine ass trap niggas." Raven giggled. She was clearly getting drunk.

"Yea, you had enough drinking for the night," Diggy said, taking her cup. Niomi giggled and now it was Raven's time to roll her eyes at Niomi.

"We about to go celebrate, we're out." Renz dapped up Diggy while Raven and Niomi briefly hugged.

Renz had gotten them a suite at the very hotel, on the same floor. Theirs was a honeymoon suite.

"You know she's right though?" Niomi asked as she walked hand and hand with Renz down the hotel hall.

"About what?" Renz asked, giving her his full attention.

"I am caught up."

"Shit, that makes the both of us. I love you, Mrs. White."

Still Caught Up With A Trap God

"I love you more Mr. White."

Chapter 1 Carmen

"You're so beautiful," Raul said, standing over me as I laid stretch out in our king size bed. I was in my pajamas, feeling ugly and swollen. My son had me feeling like I was carrying a truck inside my body instead of a baby boy. This pregnancy has been a long journey, from the morning sickness to the emotional episodes and the swelling. I was just glad it all was about to be over.

"You don't have to lie to me," I told him.

Lately, all the weight I picked up had me feeling anything but pretty. Raul titled his head back like he was offended before he walked over to the bed. He had just gotten out of the shower, so the water glistened down his six-pack. I was so turned on, I stared at him in a trance. Because of my son, my sexual relationship had been nonexistent for the last couple of months. I wanted to make love to my man, but it was too uncomfortable, and I seemed to never be in the mood.

"Carmen, you're beautiful as fuck and I'm not just saying that because you're my baby momma. I can't wait until you have my son next week," Raul said and I smiled.

Next week was my due date, but I was ready for him to come out now. I was ready for Quincy to come into this world, so I could lay eyes on my baby boy. I was ready to hold him in my arms and protect him. I was just ready to birth what we created and meet the baby boy who will always own my heart.

"Thank you. Where are you going?" I asked, noticing him putting on clothes.

"Out," he said nonchalantly and I rolled my eyes.

This was the reason I sometimes wish Raulin wasn't in the streets; he was always on the move. Truthfully, I couldn't be upset because he warned me what came with him being in the streets. At the same time, with it being so close to me having our son, I would at least think he would be home more. That's wishful thinking though. All he's been doing lately is coming home to take a shower then leaving right back out. I was beginning to question my place in his life. It felt like we weren't as important as his lifestyle. I hoped his behavior would change once our son arrived.

"You can't stay here with me tonight?"

"You going to start this again, Carmen? You know what I'm out here doing. This is how I'm going to make sure my son and us are straight."

"Okay," I said, knowing there wasn't no point in going back and forth with Raul. He wasn't staying and I knew that was final.

"Just thug it out with me, Carmen. Shit's not going to be this way forever." He gave me a kiss on the forehead and just like that, he was out the door. Wiping away the tears, I grabbed the remote off the nightstand and turned on a re-run show of *Martin* until I fell asleep.

***

"Ahhhhhhh!" I woke up crying and sweating.

Sharp pains overcame me and it was hard for me to breathe. Feeling wetness between my legs, I began to panic. Grabbing my phone, I noticed it was three in the morning, and Raul wasn't insight. Calling his phone, it rang and rang until the voicemail picked up. Calling him back again, it was the same result. After not being able to reach him, I called 911.

As I waited for the ambulance, I called Raul again and sent him a text saying I think I was in labor and to call me now. I cried tears as I rocked back and forth in agonizing pain. It took the paramedics a few minutes to get to my house and I was happy. I was happy I could unlock the gate and the front door that surrounded our home from my phone because I wasn't in any position to move. I watched as they entered my home. Raul was paranoid so he installed cameras in and outside our home and made sure the feed came to our phones.

"Ma'am, where are you in the home?" I could hear the deep, raspy voice of one of the paramedics ask.

"I'm up here!" I yelled out the best that I could. I heard footsteps coming up the stairs and it wasn't long after then two Caucasian paramedics in blue uniforms entered my room. They helped me on the gurney and I was truly thankful. I wasn't sure how long I could deal with the pain.

When I arrived at the hospital, everything seemed to be moving quickly. They brought me to the back and immediately began to hook me up to machines.

"My name is Doctor Riley and I'll be delivering your baby," the black doctor said with a smile. I smiled back because she was black. She look about 5 feet and she had natural, curly hair, She had an aura about her that made you want to smile.

"Can I get something for the pain?" I asked. The pain was too much to bare.

"I'm sorry, there's no time to administer the epidural. You're 10 centimeters dilated and it's time to have this baby. I need you to put your legs up so that your feet are flat on the bed. I need you to wait for me to say push and when I do, you push. You understand?" She asked.

"Wait, my child's father is not here. I can't be in labor alone!" I cried, petrified. This was my first child, my first pregnancy and I had no idea what to expect. I was alone and in pain. I wanted my son to be able to experience having both his parents there for his delivery. I wanted Raul to cut our son's umbilical core and I wanted his father and I to be the first people that welcome him into this world.

"I'm sorry, ma'am, there's no time to wait. Please, let's proceed." I nodded my head and she gave me a smile before putting on sterile gloves. "Just follow my lead and you'll be okay." She smiled once more and that made me feel a little better. "One, two, and three. Push."

"Ahhhhh!" I yelled as I pushed.

"You're doing great. Again, push!"

"Ahhhhhhhhh!" I screamed out in pain as I pushed again. Seconds later, I could hear the sounds of my son crying, and I cried as well.

"You have a beautiful baby boy. You want to cut the umbilical cord ?" One of the nurses asked and I nodded my head, too emotional to talk.

She handed me the scissors and I cut the cord before they took him to clean him off.

"He's 6lbs and 6oz. Do you want to hold him?" The same nurse asked.

Again, I was too emotional to answer, so I just nodded my head yes. My son cried as the nurse put him on my chest, it didn't take long for him to stop. It warmed my heart as I laid eyes on my son, who was the spitting image of his father.

Five hours. That's how long after I had Quincy that Raul came to the hospital. I was laying down watching the hospital TV. I was still in a little pain but feeling way better. My brother, Diggy, Niomi and Raven had just left. Quincy was in the hospital basinet next to my bed sleeping. I was so in love with him, I couldn't sleep because I was so overwrought about leaving my son unattended. I watch so many Lifetime movies and my son getting kidnap from the hospital wouldn't be my life.

"Baby, I'm so sorry. I just saw the messages and phone calls, I'm so sorry." Raul came rushing in the hospital room. He leaned over and kissed my head. I angrily stared at him.

"You think sorry is going to fix this? You come in here saying sorry after leaving me to give birth to our son, ALONE!" I barked and my son stirred in his sleep, causing us both to look in his direction. Raul walked over to him before looking at me then back at him.

"Damn, my little nigga look just like me and Que," he said. As much as I didn't want to, I smiled because he did.

"Wash your hands before you pick him up. Right behind you, that door is the bathroom."

He nodded his head and then headed in the direction of the bathroom. Seconds later, he was coming back. He picked up Quincy and walked around the room talking to him. I look on at the scene before me, smiling. I hated Raul for missing the birth of our son, and he was definitely going to hear my mouth later, but I wouldn't deny the fact that this moment was beautiful.

Chapter 2 Raul

Most would think since Renz gave me his business to run, shit would be easy for me to come in and continue making the money he was making. That shit was far from the truth. If anything, I was working twice as hard to keep shit a float. Niggas were testing me because they felt like this shit was given to me. They must have thought a nigga was pussy, but they found out quickly I wasn't petrified of catching a body. After having to kill three niggas for testing my gangster, niggas started to fall in line. I been putting in work in these streets and I have the money as the proof. I switched shit up from how Renz and Diggy were running it. Shit was cool when they were running shit and it worked for them, but this was my operation now and I was going to run it how I see fit.

"Boss man, any word yet?" One of my soldiers asked as we sat around in my warehouse. Tonight, was the night Meechie, my plug from Atlanta, was bringing the shipment. I just didn't know exactly what time he was coming.

Renz and Diggy were fucking with the pill shit heavy. Even though the pills were bringing in money, I decided not to fuck with that shit as heavy as they were. I had more bricks than a brick house. A nigga was out here feeding the streets with the purest drugs and although it was killing my people, I didn't give a fuck. A nigga like me didn't have a big enough heart to care about the moms, dads, brothers, sisters, or whoever I was selling work to. All I cared about was me and mines, and that's how I knew I was meant to be the leader of my own drug operation. There was no love in these streets, so I wasn't going into this shit with a heart. You had to be a callous motherfucker to get in the streets, conquer and bow out gracefully. That was the goal. At first, I thought this street shit would be it for me. That was until I saw how Diggy and Renz were living. These motherfuckers were living the life and they weren't even in the streets anymore. I wanted to leave it alone eventually, but I needed to stack up the money to get out and that shit would take years to get.

"Shit, not yet," I said. As soon as the words left my mouth, the location was coming to my phone.

"It's go fucking time, let's roll out," I told my soldiers. It was always me and three of my workers getting the shipment. These niggas were head of the traps I had them running. I trusted these niggas to a certain extent, and that's why they were able to roll with me.

Pulling up to the location, I got out the U-haul truck we used to transport the drugs. The U-haul truck was actually Renz's from the moving company he started. He now had two successful businesses: his temp service and his moving company. He was the one who brought it to my attention to use the truck to transport drugs. He said to have two niggas in the back with the product while me and the other nigga is up front. At first, I was skeptical, but once the nigga reminded me that the goal was to reman inconspicuous, then I took his advice. I couldn't deny that doing shit his way was genius. I was able to move surreptitiously and make hell of money at the same time.

Pulling up to the location where the plug was meeting me, I got out the truck with my pistol in my hand. It has been a smooth operation this far, yet I wouldn't be the nigga I was if I didn't take precautions. Plug or not, if some shit wasn't adding up, I was subtracting his ass from the problem. I didn't trust shit. One fuck up and I could be in the grave. I learned that shit from my brother's demise. I had a kid about to come into this world and a woman that needed me. I couldn't let no motherfucker get one up on me.

Seeing headlights followed by a huge ass semi-truck, I knew who it was. Glancing in the U-haul truck, my solider nodded his head. They knew not to get out the truck but to stay on point. Heading over to the truck, I opened the back door and slid into the backseat.

"Raul, what's good with you?" Meechie asked, giving me dap.

"Nothing new, trying to make more money," I said and he nodded.

"I wanted to holla at you about the numbers you been making. I see the work you putting in, little nigga. Keep the shit up and when it's time, something big will come your way," he told me and I nodded. He went on to talk about me coming down to the A, and I just told him I would with no intent on keeping my word. Columbus was my motherfucking stomping grounds. There was no point in going to the A when the ball was in my court here.

After chopping it up with Meechie, I turned off my phone and it was go time. Meechie had that pure shit, but it was up to me and my niggas to cook that bitch right. A nigga was a chef when it came to whipping up the dope. I had given the niggas under me the blueprint to how to flick the wrist when it came to cooking work.

It took us a total of five hours to get the work to all the spots and get shit organized. After I was done, a nigga was beat. It wasn't until I was heading home that I turned my phone back on and realized Carmen had been blowing me up. When I saw the text saying she was in labor, a nigga's heart dropped, and I immediately headed to the hospital. It was a whole hour ago that she sent the text, and I prayed my whole way to the hospital that she didn't have my seed without me being there. I broke every traffic law there was getting to them. When I arrived and they let me know Carmen had already delivered, a nigga felt like shit.

When the nurse walked me to the room where Carmen and Quincy were, I felt like shit. I missed the birth of my seed. I could see the hurt that danced around in the pupils of Carmen's eyes. There really wasn't shit I could say. She had all rights to be disappointed in me. Yet, a nigga had to say something. She wasn't feeling shit I was saying, but that was gravy because I'll make it up to her. After washing my hands, I walked over to my little nigga and smiled. He looked just like his uncle. My older brother, Quincy, was killed a few years back and that's who we named my son after; him, along with Carmen's oldest brother, Renz, one of my brother's best friend.

"Damn, Daddy promise I'm going to give you the world," I told my son as I stared at him pacing back and forth with him in my arms. I know he didn't understand exactly what I was saying, but the small smile he gave me was all the confirmation I needed. This grind I was about to put in the streets was for him. My son will never get to experience the struggle like I did, I'll make sure of that. I was in love with my little man. I couldn't believe when Carmen first told me she was pregnant, I didn't want her to keep my son. I was glad she did. Carmen and Quincy brought a happiness to my life I couldn't even explain.

Still Caught Up With A Trap God

***

It's been a week since my son's been born and still, Carmen was giving me the cold shoulder. Granted, I did miss the birth of my son, but a nigga was fed up when it came to her not fucking with me.

"So, you just gon' keep ignoring a nigga?" I asked, walking into the kitchen where she was standing in nothing but a t-shirt. I had a box of Ohio State pizza in my hand, knowing that was her favorite pizza. I was trying to make shit right with my girl. We had a beautiful baby boy and us being at odds was fucking up what should have been a happy moment.

"What is there really to talk about, Raulin? You missed seeing your son being brought into this world! You have been MIA since we had our son. I'm new to being a mother, and I feel all alone. Like damn, you couldn't be around for me and your son? The streets that damn important?!" She yelled, slamming the refrigerator door shut.

Putting the pizza box on the table, I shook my head at her and ran my hand down my face, mentally telling myself to calm down. I love Carmen and I could understand why she was upset, but it infuriated me that she didn't get it yet. Her man was a street nigga. I wanted my son to have everything I didn't have growing up. I wanted the both of them to be straight for life, so a nigga was out here working overtime. She should have understood that shit. She was talking like a nigga wanted to miss my son being born or that I wanted to be away as much.

"Look, I'm just trying to provide for you and my son. What the fuck you want from me, Carmen? Damn, I'm just trying to make sure we're straight and don't want for shit else. I'm here now and I'm trying. I'm about to go get my son and you can bring the pizza upstairs. I'm trying to spend time with my family. Make sure you leave the attitude down here."

I gave her a kiss and then walked away from her ass. She looked at me angrily, but I wasn't worried. Shit, her ass better have a different mood when she come up these stairs. Going to the room we had set up for my son, I went over to his crib and picked him up. When I grabbed him, his eyes opened and when they landed on me, he smiled.

"What's up, little man, you miss your dad?" I asked and he smiled more.

"Damn, you look so much like your uncle. I love you, little man. You're about to come chill with me and your stuck-up ass momma." Grabbing his basinet with one hand and carrying him in the other, I headed to our bedroom. Carmen was there and she had the pizza.

"Let me get my baby." She held out her arms.

"Nah, he chilling with his pops right now," I said and she rolled her eyes.

"I told you leave that attitude shit downstairs, Carmen. Put something on the T.V," I told her and she did what I asked. Hearing my phone ring, I glanced down and pressed ignore, only for the caller to call right back.

"I can't talk right now," I said and then hung up. Glancing up from looking at my son, I looked into Carmen's questioning eyes.

"Who was that?"

"Business."

"Turn off your phone, it's supposed to be family time," she said and I agreed.

I did what I needed to do at the traps. I collected my money and brought it to the stash spot. I gave niggas more work, so my phone shouldn't ring. Turning off my phone, I laid back and kicked it with my family.

Chapter 3 Carmen

Post-partum depression was something I'd seen women talking about after having a child but didn't take any of them serious. I thought it was just something females said, now I was learning first-hand how serious the feeling of depression was after becoming a new mother, or a mother in general. It didn't help that Raulin was in the streets heavily. I thought when Quincy came, he would want to be around more, but it was like our son being born ignited the grind in him. Before I woke up in the morning, he was gone and he always came in after I was sleep. The only reason I knew he was there is because I could feel when he got in bed. Raulin and I didn't have the best relationship starting off. Honestly speaking, he wasn't too pleased to find out I was pregnant. Yet, even after he played me, had me crying over him, causing my brother and I to be on the odds and denying my baby, I still gave him a chance. Things eventually got better between us, but here I was, feeling like I did when we first started messing around. Like I was the only one putting an effort in.

I laid in bed feeling lethargic. I could hear Quincy fussing, but I was literally too tired to move. I have been up late nights and early mornings with him. I'd been feeling so overwhelmed and crying so much, I've been having migraines for days. I wanted to call my brother so bad, but the last thing I wanted to do is cause an altercation between him and Raulin, especially since they hashed out their issues recently. I just wish Raulin would step up as a father and a man.

"You don't hear my fucking son? Get your ass up!" I could hear Raulin's voice. He must've just got in because he wasn't here a minute ago.

"You get him, act like a fucking father for once!" I barked. He look at me before he left out the room.

My son's room was the next over, so I could hear him talking to my son. He was still crying and I could hear Raulin asking him what's wrong. Heading downstairs, I made him a bottle and gave it to Raulin.

"He's hungry. Make sure you're holding his head and bottle right when feeding him."

"I don't need you to tell me how to hold my damn son. Your unfit ass was about to let him starve."

"Nigga, shut up. I'm here day in and day out with MY son, your ass barely sees him. He probably don't even know your stupid ass."

"You mad as hell a nigga making sure your funky ass don't need or want for shit. Damn, a nigga providing for his family and your ass complaining. If a motherfucker wasn't grinding, then it would still be a problem. Be happy and shut the fuck up!"

"Fuck you, Raulin!" I yelled and walked out of my son's room. Going to my bedroom, I got dressed and headed out the house to go to my brother's.

Ten minutes into the drive, Raul was blowing my phone up.

"What?"

"Where the fuck your dumb ass go?"

"Nigga, don't worry about it. Spend time with your son for once!" I told him and hung up the phone. Knowing he was going to call again, I turned off my phone and headed to my brother's.

Pulling up to Renz's, I smiled. He moved since the last house I shared with him. This home was bigger and I was more than proud of him. What was more satisfying is the fact he paid for it the legal way. Couldn't nobody, especially the police, come and take what is his. Parking the car, I got out and knocked on the door. I knew he would be looking at the camera, him or Niomi. If they were here, they would see me, so I looked up and smiled.

"What your big ass doing here?" I heard Renz through the intercom.

"Let me in!" I whined because his ass was always playing. It was April and the weather was nice, but I didn't want to be out here waiting.

Hearing the door unlock, I was met by Renz.

"Give big bro a hug. How your ass been, stranger?" He asked. Giving him a hug, I kissed his cheek, walked in and sat on his all red, Italian sofa.

"I'm not a stranger."

"Yes, your ass is. Where's my nephew?"

"I left him with his damn daddy. He needs to be home with him for once."

"What's all that animosity in your voice? You want to talk about some shit?"

"I do, but the last thing I want is for you to feel some kind of way about Raul because of our situation."

"I told you, baby sis, I'm going to let you be a woman. As long as the nigga not putting his hands on you, we're good. You're my baby sister and a nigga will always be a listening ear."

"I just feel like Raul is putting the streets above our family. He said he is grinding for us, but what's the purpose of grinding if the grind is only for the materialistic shit and not anything more? Like the house, clothes, shoes, bags and money, none of that means anything to me if my son doesn't know his father."

"I get that, baby sis, but if I'm being honest, you knew what you were signing up for. Now before you say something, hear me out. The streets are deadly. I'm saying if you don't stay on your P's and Q's, you can take a L and sometimes that L means your freedom or even worse, your life. I'm not agreeing with Raul's choice of being in the streets more than he's with his family, but what I will say is I get it. Before, it was just you and him, now he has a whole child to provide for. That shit is on the back of his mind while he's out there. He's trying to stack enough money so his son never wants for anything. Take it easy on the little nigga because after being in them grimy streets all day, he needs to come home to peace. "

"I should have known you would take his side."

"Chill out with that shit, you know I'll never put a soul before you. I'm just being one hunnit with you. If you ever need a break, you know you can bring nephew over here. Niomi and I won't mind keeping him for you."

"I appreciate you. How's Niomi? Has her memory started to come back yet?"

"Nah, I can't help but to still feel guilty over that shit. If I didn't lie to her, she probably wouldn't have half her life erased from her mental. That shit bothers me every day."

"You can't change the past, all you can do is learn from your mistakes."

"Look at your big-headed ass sounding educated and all grown up. You want to stay for dinner? Niomi will be back shortly. We haven't seen you since you gave birth and even then, we didn't get to talk as much as I wanted. I miss you."

"I miss you too, I would love to stay," I told Renz. Raul would have to just be mad and cancel any plans he had. I needed a break. I was more than excited to kick it with my brother and my sister-in-law, Niomi.

Chapter 4 Raul

"I'm going to strangle that damn girl," I told myself, checking the time on my phone.

Four hours Carmen has been gone, and she ain't even have the decency of calling my phone and checking on our son. That was some dead-beat mother shit right there. On top of her ass getting ghost, she had me missing out on money. This wasn't the time for her to be playing games, I was on a time limit. I was ready to stack as much money as I can before my Karma came back around and took me away from my son in the form of imprisonment or death.

Hearing the alarm say front door, I headed down the stairs to see Carmen coming in. She looked at me, gave me a smile then rolled her eyes.

"How was daddy and son time?"

"That was some fucked up in shit you did, Carmen!"

"Boy, be quiet. It did not kill you to spend half a day with your damn child."

32

"I had to make moves and you made me miss out on money."

"Nigga, so the fuck what! The streets could wait. Your son should be more important!"

"He is more important. You and him are the reason I'm out in the streets risking my freedom and my life, Carmen! Damn, stop stressing a nigga out, and just be the rider I need you to be."

"I need you to be a father. I need help, Raulin, especially since I'll be going back to school in a few more weeks."

"Back to school?"

"Yea, why are you acting so shocked? we talked about this when I told you about my plans when I was pregnant, and you agreed to it."

"Wait until Quincy gets a little older to think about that shit."

"Are you serious?"

"Yea, damn! I'm out. He ate two hours ago and I gave him a bath. He's been sleep for an hour, so he might sleep through the night."

Not waiting for her to say anything, I left out the house and hopped in my Range Rover, heading to the first of the few traps I had. Silence lingered. I was in deep thought as me and Carmen's relationship weighed heavy on my mind. I could feel us drifting apart and that was just some shit a nigga didn't want. I used to dog Carmen's ass out when she first came to me about her being pregnant. That was because she was just a fuck to me in my plot to get revenge on Renz before we became cool. Either way, I fell in love with her ass and I couldn't imagine her or my seed not being in my life. They're my purpose for being out in the streets as heavy as I was. I wish Carmen understood the grind was for us. Instead, she was stressing a nigga out. Saying fuck the trap right now, I headed to the one person I knew who would keep it real with me.

"What you doing here?" My best friend, Diamond, asked when she came to the door.

"Man, watch out. A nigga not welcome now?"

"You know your big-headed ass is welcome here anytime. What's good, stranger? I ain't see you in some weeks. You hungry?" Diamond asked. She was wearing little ass shorts and a tank top and her titties and ass were sitting right. Diamond and I used to fuck around and only ended because she wanted to call it quits. Me being the nigga I was, I didn't put up a fight. Pussy was easy for a nigga like me to get, but a real friend was something rare and that's what Diamond was to me.

"Hell yea, I could eat. Shit, you know Carmen had the baby, so a nigga been grinding over time."

"Congratulations, how's life with a new baby?" She asked, bringing me a plate of spaghetti and then sitting on the red sofa next to me.

"Shit stressful. Me and Carmen been going at it like cats and dogs. Shit crazy as fuck. She's complaining about me being gone and her being alone. Man, if I would have known shit would be like this, I would have waited a little longer before getting her ass pregnant," I told her, shaking my head.

"Well, are you gone all the time?"

"Shit, no more than how much I used to be."

"Well then, be home more. She's new to being a mother, I'm sure you not being around to help her is stressing her out."

"I should have known your ass would say some shit like that. Women love to stick together."

"Don't even try to play me like that. You know I'm team you, but I wouldn't be me if I didn't keep it a hunnit with you when your ass fucks up."

"Yea, I hear you. Go get a bottle of some good shit you got and roll this wood up for me," I told her.

She didn't say anything, but she headed to the back and I knew she was doing what I asked her to do. That's why I fucked with Diamond. She was one of those women who did what a nigga asked. If Carmen didn't have a nigga's heart, I wouldn't have mind making Diamond my girl. We'd been friends since I was a knucklehead on the block. She was the shorty every nigga wanted and nobody could get. A nigga as cocky as myself knew I could get her. She had me feeling just as salty as them niggas when she played my ass. I never gave up though. We eventually became friends until we got a little older and started fucking. Shorty was one hunnit. I fuck with her and had mad love for her.

"What you been up to though? You gave any of these fuck niggas a chance yet?"

"Nah, the pussy maybe," she joked as she laughed by herself. I stared at her and my silence made to look up from her phone.

"What... you jealous? You miss the pussy?" She threw another shot back.

"Shit, what if I do?" I asked.

The liquor was getting to me and although I know what I was doing is wrong, I didn't give a fuck. Diamond and I just had a vibe, and the sexual chemistry was there. Carmen wasn't fucking with a nigga. On top of that, I haven't been getting no pussy and I was feeling back up. She was on that six-week time out. Even before she had Quincy, we weren't fucking because the shit was too painful for her. Yea, shit wasn't right, but I'm a man and I need some pussy.

"You're drunk, you need to leave."

"So, you kicking me out now?" I asked, standing up. Even though she just told me to leave, the lascivious stare she gave me told me all I needed to know. Dropping my pants, my dick stood at attention, waiting for her to bless him.

"Damn, what the fuck? That shit won't stop growing," Diamond said she got in front of it and begin to slurp on my shit like it was an ice pop or some shit. I ran my hand through her shoulder length, sandy brown hair and bit down on my bottom lip. Diamond was a freak. Not only did she have good pussy, she had good ass head.

Humming on my dick, she began to make it really sloppy. She moved both her hands around my dick in a circular motion as she spit on it. She did that a few more times before she removed one of her hands and replaced it with her mouth. Looking up at me, she sucked on my balls, never stopping massaging my dick. She looked me in the eyes and no lie, a nigga was scared. This bitch was a demon, and she was handling the dick too well.

"Damn, Diamond." A nigga was about to slide her ass, that's how good she was sucking my dick. She giggled and stood up. I didn't say shit. I was about to nut and once I did, I was out. I'll be lying if I said I didn't want to sample the pussy like it was a nigga 's appetizer.

"Bend that ass over," I told her, going into my jeans and retrieving a magnum. She did what I asked and I slid right into the pussy like it was home base on a baseball field. She moaned out and I had to pause before I continued to beat her shit up like a nigga was trying to go to jail for domestic violence.

"Damn, Raul. Damn, hold up." She tried to push me away, but a nigga was in beast mode. I was backed up and taking out all my anger on her pussy.

"You can't handle the dick no more, Diamond?" I asked her as I began to smack her ass. She started to throw her ass back on a nigga, and I nodded my head in approval. This is why I fuck with Diamond. She welcomed the aggressive sex that I like to have. The magnum ended up breaking but I kept going. The shit was feeling to good to stop.

An hour later, I was nutting inside of her.

"You on birth control, right?"

"Yea, I can't let a nigga come and baby daddy me," she said, sticking out her tongue. I headed to the back, shaking my head at her crazy ass. Getting a rag, I cleaned myself off, and she walked in the bathroom a few seconds later to do the same.

"That was fun." She rubbed on my dick and I looked at her. I couldn't help but to think about Carmen. From the beginning, I was playing her. From just fucking her to denying my son and having secret agendas when it came to her. I kept fucking up. Deep down, I knew she was too good for me, but I couldn't see her fucking with no nigga that wasn't me. Looking at Diamond, I kissed her head before exiting the bathroom then leaving the house. My next destination was my traps.

Going to the first one, I walked in, giving them niggas the surprise of their life. Nobody knew when I was going to just pop up. I didn't trust the idea of niggas knowing when I was coming. I just tried to do some grimy shit to Renz and Diggy by stealing money from their trap. A nigga would be a fool to think some shit like that couldn't happen to me. When I walked in the trap, niggas were on they shit though.

"What's good, bossman. You know that nigga Rich Boy came by today?"

"That nigga Rich Boy?" I asked, cocking my head slightly back. I haven't talk to that nigga since he called himself rolling up on Carmen at her school. Nigga was on some snake shit and I wasn't fucking with him. It was fucked up because he used to be my right-hand. He wasn't feeling me wanting to give back the money to Renz and Diggy. On some sucker shit, the nigga got ghost, so him coming around is a red flag like a motherfucker.

"Yea, he tried to see what's happening in the trap. I shut that shit down though 'cause I haven't seen y'all together in a minute."

"Yea, good job staying on your P's and Q's. Next time the nigga come back around, make sure you hit my line," I told him. He nodded his head and I headed in the back. I went into the bedroom on the right, which is consider our money room. Two of my soldiers were in the room dapping them up. I sat back watching how my young nigga, Dub, put the money in the counter, wrapped it in rubber bands then passed it to Kilo who was putting money under the floorboard. I nodded my head in approval cause them niggas were on their shit. After staying for another hour to supervise the transaction and how shit was running, I went to my next trap and did the same thing. By the time I was done, it was late as hell. Not wanting to argue with Carmen tonight about coming home late, I decided to just get a hotel to crash at. I was tired and needed to rest. I've been on go mode for weeks, only getting a few hours of sleep.

I woke up at nine in the morning with hell of missed calls from Carmen. Shaking my head, I blew out a frustrated breath before calling her back.

"You straight?" I asked when she picked up the phone.

"So, we staying out all night now, Raulin!?" She screamed.

"I was tired. I just crashed at a hotel. I'm on my way back now." I hung up, not waiting for her response. I knew it was going to be some shit. That was one of the rules Carmen had, always come home every night.

"Where you at, Carmen?" I called out to her when I came into the house.

Not getting a response, I headed upstairs. First stop I made was my son's room. Heading over to his crib, I saw him lying on his back and I smiled. My little nigga really made me a dad. Leaning down, I kissed him before heading into my bedroom. I could hear the sniffling noise and I ran my hand down my face. Getting in the bed, I wrapped my arms around Carmen and kissed the back of her neck a few times.

"What you in here crying and shit for?"

"I can't do this anymore, Raulin."

"What you talking about, Carmen? Turn around and talk to me."

She did and when I saw her face, a nigga felt like shit. Her eyes were red and puffy, and white lines stained her cheeks from the dried-up tears. I wasn't sure why she was crying, but either way, I dropped the ball. It was clear Carmen was hurting over some shit. I hated to see her hurt. As her man, all I wanted was to give her happiness, money and my seeds. All the pain and worry she may have had, I was going to carry that shit on my back.

"I'm talking about us! I'm taking my baby and getting out of here. I'm not happy! You're coming in late and now you're not coming home at all. You're leaving me to go through parenthood on my own! I have to go through the fact I no longer feel beautiful alone. I'm not stupid, Raulin, I know there's someone else. You're not no father no way, so I'm going to take Quincy and you will never hear from us again."

Laughing was the only reaction a nigga could give her. It wasn't a funny laugh, more like a chuckle. She was on some psychotic shit if she thought I was about to let her and my son just walk out my life.

"Who the fuck else is it going to be, Carmen? I keep telling you, I'm grinding. Fuck happened to you? You became more of a fucking headache after having my son. I'm going to warn your ass right now! Leave out of here like you moving out with my son and I'ma fuck your ass up!"

"I'm going through post-partum depression and it's like you don't even give a fuck. Why are you holding me hostage in a relationship you never wanted from the beginning anyway?"

"So, we bringing up old shit? The fuck is postpartum depression. I'm doing all I can, damn! You want to be in the hood, struggling to get by, not having shit to eat, praying for your next meal? This fucking lifestyle comes with a price, and the price is me risking my fucking freedom and life. The price is me hustling from the sun up to the sun down. The price is me coming in late! You agreed to the shit. How the fuck are you going to start complaining about some shit I talked to you about while you were pregnant?"

"Nigga, you think if you come in earlier and spend more time with your family, we will live in the hood? Nigga, please. First off, my brother would never let that happen."

"Your brother?" I asked, cocking my head back, slightly offended. Yea, Carmen had me fucked up in here.

"Your brother's not going to let that happen? I'm not going to let that shit happen! I'm a muthafucking man, ain't nobody else about to take care of my fucking family but me! Carmen, I'm trying just like you are. What the fuck you want me to do? You think you're the only one stressing? The fucking weight of the world is on my shoulders. Don't you get that one fuck up can take me away from y'all forever! It takes one fuck up, just one, for me to go from coming into the crib late to me not coming back at all!" I didn't mean to yell at her, but shit, she had a nigga irate as fuck right now. I thought having a baby was going to bring us closer together, but in reality, it was only making us fall apart. This shit was not how I pictured it to be.

"Ok, Raulin. Make love to me," she said and I looked at her.

"What? The doctor said-"

"I don't care what the doctor said, I want to feel beautiful. I want you to make love to me. That's the least you can do."

"I don't think that's a good idea," I told her and I regretted it as soon as I said it. The look on her face pulled at a nigga's heart strings.

"So, you don't think I'm beautiful anymore and there's someone else. I'm not dumb but okay, Raulin, just get out." She sat on the bed looking in another direction and didn't look my way again.

"You know you beautiful as fuck to me, and there's not nobody else. Come take a shower with me," I told her.

She got up and followed me to the bathroom. Adjusting the water for us, I stripped down and then took off the t-shirt she was wearing. Even with the small pudge she had and the stretch marks, she was beautiful as fuck to me. Getting in the shower, I began to wash up before I washed her up. Looking at Carmen, I wanted to fuck her. A nigga felt guilty 'cause I was just in some pussy that wasn't hers last night, but I couldn't have her feeling as if a nigga didn't find her attractive. Sliding into Carmen, I began to fuck her. We hadn't had sex in a while and a nigga forgot how good the pussy was.

"Damn, Carmen, this pussy good," I grunted in her ear. Carmen had the kind of pussy to make a nigga want to nut inside her and after fucking the shit out of her, I did.

"What the fuck, Raulin! I'm not on birth control, we need to definitely get a pill."

"Shit, if you end up pregnant, that's what the fuck it is. I don't give a fuck, let's have a big family." I shrugged, washing us both up before stepping out the shower.

Wrapping a towel around me, I did the same to her when she stepped out.

"We definitely don't need another child." She look at me disgusted.

"What you give me that look for? You ready to start with that bullshit again," I told her, shaking my head and heading out the bathroom. She followed behind me. I ignored her ass and proceeded to get dress.

"We don't need another kid, you barely see the son we do have. That'll be two kids growing up to feel abandoned by their father."

I wanted to smack the fuck out of Carmen, but I would never disrespect her stupid ass like that. Instead, I did the only thing a nigga could do. I got dressed and went back out in the streets to grind. There was no peace at home and it was fucked up. Being a nigga in the streets, all you want to do is come home to peace in your crib. Pushing the shit me and Carmen were going through to the back of my head, I got in demon mode. That's how I had to be out here so a nigga won't catch me slipping. It was a deadly game out here, and I wish Carmen understood that shit.

Chapter 5 Rich Boy

Eat or get eaten has always been a motto for me. Growing up, I didn't have shit; not a pot to piss in or a window to throw it out of. I never knew either one of my parents. They dropped me off at the nearest fire station and a nigga had been jumping from foster care to foster care since. Every time I got adopted, the family would return me. It was fucked up, but those are the cards I was dealt in life, so I played the fuck out of the shit. I was a hotheaded nigga and that's all a nigga knew how to be. Growing up in different foster homes, wasn't shit easy. I had to fight to survive and I had to rob to eat. Shit, robbing niggas is how I met Raul. Raul was my nigga back in the day, but the nigga went soft. He got on some cool shit with them niggas Renz and Diggy. I didn't respect that shit, so it was fuck that nigga. Riding down the street, I shook my head as I thought back to the day that punk-ass Detective Johnson pulled me over.

I was riding down the street with my girl and she was fussing about some bitch she caught me fucking with.

"So, you're still texting the bitch? She worth losing everything we built?"

"Man, do your ass ever stop nagging? You mad over a bitch texting my damn phone when I come home to you every night. I fuck you good and I give you money, fuck you whining for, damn! Give me my phone!" I barked, snatching my damn phone out her hand.

Here a nigga was about to take her on a date, and she started with this nagging shit. Her snatching my phone out my hand, and smacking me in my face 'caused me to swerve. As soon as I did, the sound of sirens could be heard. Looking in the rearview mirror, I noticed the flashing lights on the black car. Shaking my head, I pulled over. I glared at Rissa, wanting to slap the shit out of her; a nigga was hot right now. With the money I took from Renz and Diggy, I brought me some coke and been putting that white devil in the streets. Today was reup day and I had a trunk full of the shit. I was on my way to my spot where I held this shit and a nigga was shitting bricks. The brown-skinned detective walked to my side of the car and tapped on the window, so I rolled it down.

"Richard Benjamin, can you step out of the car, please?"

"What's this all about, detective?" I asked, looking at his badge. I was skeptical because this nigga already knew who I was and that shit didn't sit right with me.

"Step out the car, both of you, and sit on the curve." This time, his voice held a little more authority in it. As bad as I wanted to say fuck this nigga, I didn't. The last thing I wanted was for my bitch to see me get shot down like a dog in the street by the police. Doing what he said, he cuffed me, then headed back over to where my car was I watched as he searched the car, and I prayed like hell he didn't check the truck.

"Fuck is your warrant, nigga?"

"Shut up!" He said, pulling out his gun and aiming it at me. Rissa screamed and cried. I glared at her.

When we first got pulled, I thought the shit was her fault. If she would have kept her hands to herself, we wouldn't have gotten pulled over. The fact that this hoe ass detective knew my name, I knew he had secret intent. I watched as he headed to my trunk. The smile he had on his face when he opened it let me know he hit the jackpot. Hanging my head, I just shook it. I was about to go to jail.

A nigga got caught red-handed with a trunk full of that white girl.

"Well looka here." The detective came over to me smirking. *"You know that can put you in jail for at least 20 years."*

"Fuck you."

"Now is that a way to talk to someone who can keep this a secret and guarantee your freedom?"

"What are you talking about?"

"I know you're connected to Lorenzo White, Damonte Carter, and Raulin Thomas. Also known as Renz, Diggy, and Raul."

"I don't be with them niggas."

"Come on, Rich Boy, you think I don't know all about y'all. You want to be free, you will help me."

"Man, what you need?"

"Where's your phone?"

"In the cupholder in the car."

I watched as he went over to my car and grabbed my phone. He came back and stood above me with my phone still in his hand."

"What's your passcode?" Giving it to him, I watched as he typed some shit in and a few minutes later, his phone was ringing.

"I'll be in touch." He uncuffed me, smiled at Rissa, then headed to his car.

"Don't tell me you're actually considering being a rat," Rissa said when we got in the car.

"What else am I supposed to do?"

That was a week ago and yesterday, Detective Robinson called, telling me it was time to bring him something that could lock all them niggas up. I told the nigga about the bank hits and still, he wanted proof. I wasn't sure how I was going to prove that shit, so I decided to just stop by where Raul's traps. I was going to play it cool with his soldiers and try to get as much information as I could out of them niggas, but they shut my ass down, leaving me with shit. It was fucked up because now a nigga had nothing. Detective Robinson was on my ass about bringing some solid proof on everything I had going on, and my bitch wasn't fucking with me because a nigga turned state. Life was fucked up right now, but I ain't have no control. If I didn't turn rat, I would be sitting in a cell for them jersey numbers and I refused to do that. I wasn't sure what my game plan was, but I would figure that shit out.

Chapter 6 Niomi

"**P**ush, baby, push. She's almost here," Renz said, holding my hand. The pain I felt was indescribable.

"I can't, it hurts!" I cried as I squeezed his hand.

"You can, baby, just one push, just keep pushing," he told me, kissing me. I listened to the doctor as she told me to push with all my might.

"Ahhhhhh!" I screamed and pushed with all my might. Seconds later, I could hear crying coming from my child. I cried because the sound of her voice was like music to my ears. I watched Renz cut the umbilical cord then follow the doctor and nurses as they cleaned up my baby. Seconds later, they were putting her on my chest.

"6lbs 7oz, baby girl. Congratulations. Have you thought of any names?"

"Amara, Jaliyah Carmen White," Renz answered and I smiled.

"That's a beautiful name," the nurse said, and I smiled at her.

The doctor and nurses continued to clean under me. I watched as they took Amara away and Renz followed behind her. I smiled and closed my eyes. Giving birth took a toll on my body.

***

Hearing the sounds of Amara, I woke up to see Detective Robinson holding my daughter in his arms.

"Detective Robinson, what are you doing in my room with my daughter." I panicked. I hadn't seen him since the conversation we had at the restaurant months back. I wasn't sure how he knew where I was and that had me scared. It's obvious he'd been keeping tabs on me and I wasn't sure why.

"She's beautiful like her mother," he said, rocking her back and forth. He looked back at me and I tried to reach for her, but he moved back slightly.

"You know, Niomi, I don't see how someone so beautiful can be so dumb," he said with a slight chuckle followed by shaking his head.

"Excuse me?" I asked, never taking my eyes off my daughter. I went to reach for the button to call for help, but he snatched it out of my hand.

"You really would be with a man who, along with his friends, held a gun, and pointed it in your face. You were so shook, you couldn't sleep. You really would be with the man who caused you all that pain and grief?" He looked at me in disappointment.

I glared at him in anger. I was getting psychotic stalker vibes from him. Like, how the hell did he know I was at this hospital and just had a baby? He was sick and I wasn't sure how I would deal with him. I mean, it wasn't like I could just call the police on him; he was the police.

"I have no idea what you're talking about," I said as I reached for my daughter again.

He put her in my arms before reaching down and kissing my forehead. Chills flowed down my spine and I couldn't help but shed tears. I was terrified.

"You lost your memory, but I know you aren't stupid. He will go to jail and when he does, I'll be there to lean on just like I was the first time." He stared at me and

Amara, smiled at me, then walked away. Soon as he was out the door, I broke down in tears and pressed the help button. My nurse walked in immediately.

"What's wrong, Mrs. White?" She asked.

I shook my head, still trying to process Detective Robinson coming in my hospital room. I shook in fear as I held my daughter, to hysterical to talk.

"Calm down, Mrs. White, please, and let me know exactly what the problem is."

"Call my husband!"

"Is everything okay.?" She asked again.

"Just call my husband!" I screamed, causing Aamra to cry and the nurse to jump. Holding my daughter tightly, I rocked her back and forth trying to soothe her.

Chapter 7 Renz

When I got that phone call from the nurse telling me something was wrong with Niomi, I hauled ass back to the hospital. Only reason a nigga left is because I needed to shower. When I came into the room and saw MiMi crying, a nigga saw red. I was ready to body anybody in fucking sight.

"MiMi, talk to me, what's wrong?" I asked, rushing to the side of the hospital bed. She looked at me and squeezed our daughter tighter as she cried harder. "Calm down, baby. I can't fix it if I don't know what's wrong," I told her, kissing her on the forehead.

"Detective Robinson was here. I woke up to him holding Amara."

After she told me that, I called the doctor and nurse in the room.

"How can we help you, Mr White?" The doctor asked.

"I need her discharge papers, we're leaving."

"We recommend her going home tomorrow."

"I don't give a fuck what you recommend! Someone just came into my wife's room and put their hands on my daughter. Y'all failed as a hospital to protect her and her rights! Get her fucking discharge papers so we can be out!"

I got Amara and MiMi settled in at home and then had Raul come sit with them just for her sanity. The next place I headed was that bitch ass nigga's job. Police or not, a nigga didn't play when it came to mine. It was seven in the morning, but that ain't stop my ass from heading down to that damn Police station.

"Hello, sir, how may I help you?" The brown-skin police officer asked. The bitch ain't even bother to smile. I didn't give a fuck about her attitude though. If the bitch knew what was best for her, she wouldn't fuck with me when I was in this state of mind. I was ready to catch a body and I was crazy enough to kill a pig. Right now, I was like a shark who smelled blood. I was on the haunt and any fucking body would do.

"Where's Detective Robinson?"

"Sir, he took some time off."

"Well, what's his address?"

"Sir, I can't just hand out his address. If you like, I can get someone else to help you. We have plenty of detectives who are more than capable of assisting." Not bothering to respond, I left. There was no point of me being there if the hoe ass nigga wasn't there.

For the last couple of months, a nigga been a legit business man. I had a successful temp agency and was in the mist of opening another one. I had a successful moving company, became a family man and left all that street shit alone. A nigga was everything I always dreamed to be. I took that blood money and turned it to some shit that would give my family comfortability. I was setting up success for generations. Some shit I didn't have to worry about the feds coming and taking. Some shit I could leave for my daughter one day and she could do what she wanted with it. I wanted to leave all the street shit in the past, but it was shit like the situation with the detective had the demon that resided in me ready to resurface again.

Taking out my phone, I called one of the little niggas I used to have find anyone for me.

"Mike Mike, what's good."

"Aint' shit, what's up, OG? How's that legal money?"

"Better, little nigga. Say the word and I'll get you a job."

"You know a nigga like me not the type to just work. A nigga like me meant to be trapping. I was born to be a hustler."

"A hustler ain't based on your choice of job, but the choice of drive to get the income."

"Damn, you stay making niggas feel like shit when you get on that preaching shit."

"That's never my intent. I just like to educate my little niggas. Don't want to see y'all making some of the mistakes I made."

"Shit, it seems like you got it made. A beautiful wife, a family, that legal money. Don't have to worry about no damn police coming, your shit cornrow tight."

"Yea, I paid a price to get all this shit though. On another note, I need you to get as much information as you can on someone for me."

"Say less… who is it?"

"Detective Robinson. He works at the precinct right there on the ave by northern lights."

"Damn, twelve?"

"I'll make it worth your while, I need this shit done asap though."

"Alright, I got you," he said and I hung up.

I know a lot of people probably thought I was bat shit crazy going after a damn detective, but I didn't give a fuck. Yea, that badge made the nigga powerful, but I was even more powerful. That nigga fucked up putting his hands and lips on what belongs to me. I killed niggas for less. Just because he was a detective that didn't mean shit. The only thing it meant is I would have to calculate my moves when dealing with this nigga. The last thing I wanted was to get caught killing a cop being taken away from my wife and babygirl for years. Nah, I wouldn't be that dumb. Either way it goes, Detective Robinson's number was up and the nigga will get dealt with.

Chapter 8 Raven

Motherhood was something new to me and I was now a mother to two kids. A beautiful baby girl who looks just like me and a handsome little boy who looks like his father. Jr wasn't my son biologically, but you couldn't tell. I was the only mother he knew since his trifling ass mother left him at the hospital and was found dead a few weeks later. I love him like he came from my body.

Raising two kids wasn't easy, but it was a lot easier because Diggy was around and helping. He had opened up his mechanic shops since he had a thing for cars and it was doing well. So well that he was in the process of opening up his third shop. I was so proud of the man he had become.

"What do you have planned for the day?" Diggy asked, coming into the kids' room. I was in the process of getting Jr, dressed since I already got Raina dressed. In two months, Jr. would be one and Raina would be one right after.

"I'm going to visit Niomi and the baby today. What about you?"

"Looking at the location for the next shop."

"I thought you already had the location."

"I did, but it's close by the others. I'm thinking about putting one out in like Pickerington or New Albany, get some of that white money; you know shit is higher out there. I can make a killing."

"Yes, that's smart. I'm so proud of you. I just want to thank you for leaving behind all that street shit. I know you been in the streets since before we met and it wasn't easy to make that change. I feel like I don't tell you this enough, but I really appreciate you."

"You know I'll give up anything to keep you happy. I love the fuck out of you and worship you. I know it ain't easy raising a kid I made on you. I see the love you have for my son and I just want to say I appreciate that shit. Most women would just say fuck it and leave, but you never folded on a nigga, and you're the reason I go so hard. I want you to have the world and I'm going to be the nigga to bring it to your feet." He gave me a kiss and I stared in his eyes. I could see the truth in them. Yea, Diggy had made some mistakes in the past, but the past was the past and our future was brighter, so I forgave him. I've loved him since I was fifteen and I couldn't imagine loving any other man.

"You're perfect," I told him, running my hand through his curly hair.

"Nah, your chocolate ass is. I love you though. Let me know when y'all make it to Niomi's."

When I heard the door shut, I returned the phone call I missed. I hated to lie to my husband about what exactly my plans were for today, but Diggy would be livid if he knew who I was in communication with and why.

Pulling up to the meet up spot, the park, I looked around. Seeing who I was here to meet, I grabbed the double stroller out the trunk of the car before grabbing the kids out their car seat and putting them in it. Walking over to the bench where he sat waiting, I took a seat.

"Thank you for letting me see my nephew," he said. I look over at Laura's brother and nodded my head. I took Jr out the stroller and held him in my arms while I glanced at Raina still sleeping.

"Yea, I think it's time to tell Diggy we have met up a few times. I'm not really feeling letting you see Jr. without my husband's knowledge."

"That's fine with me, I'm just glad I get the opportunity to see my nephew." He gave me a quick smile and took Jr. out my arms. I watched as he bounced him up and down in his lap.

It was spring time in Ave, so it was a nice day. I glanced around at all the kids as they played with their parents and couldn't help but to smile. I love kids. They were so innocent, I couldn't understand how people could hurt them.

"How do you feel about me taking him for a week or so?" Logan asked, bringing attention back to him.

I looked at him like he was crazy. He had to be out of his mind to think I would let him just take Jr. Logan contacted me a month or so ago on Facebook. He had pics of him and Laura and said he wanted to just see his nephew. He tugged at my heart strings when he said Jr. was the only family he had since Laura met her demise. I couldn't stand that bitch Laura, but I wasn't a callous woman. Family was everything to me, so after letting him

be on FaceTime and seeing Jr., I concurred to letting him
see him. But, I didn't know him and would never let my
son out of my sight to go with him.

"Are you crazy? Didn't I just tell you I have to tell
my husband. I can't just let our son go with you." I took Jr.
out his arms because it was time to go. We'd already been
out here for too long. We were at the park, not too far away
from our house and my nerves were getting the best of me.
Everyone stayed talking about people in the hood, but
nobody spoke on how nosey the white people are. They
would be quick to say they saw me out with another man.

"That's not my problem. I want my nephew, you
handle your shit, and we'll be in touch," Logan said,
standing up from the bench.

For the first time since talking to Logan, I saw the
dark side he had. It wasn't much about what he said, but
how he said it. His words caused chills to arise on my body.
I wasn't sure I would let Logan see Jr. anymore, the vibe
was off. Getting the kids together, I decided I wouldn't
mention anything to Diggy. I was going to just go ahead
and block Logan. It was clear trying to let him have some
kind of relationship with Jr. was a bad mistake.

Still Caught Up With A Trap God

Chapter 9 Diggy

I wouldn't be keeping it one hunnit if I said putting all the street shit behind me was easy. That shit was all a nigga knew how to do, and it was fast money. That shit wasn't worth my wife's happiness, so I left the shit alone. Well, I left what I did alone. I wasn't robbing banks, armour trucks or selling drugs anymore.

"What's good, nigga?" Raulin came into my office. He threw down the two duffle bags and dapped me up.

"Ain't shit, how you living?"

"Nigga, getting richer everyday, no complaints from me."

"Real shit, how much you got for me today?"

"100k"

"Say less. Be easy out there, little nigga."

"Always. Let me ask you something."

"What's up, little nigga?" I sat back in my chair and glanced at Raul. It took me a minute to start fucking with him again after he got Carmen pregnant and was stealing from us. He did give the money back. That, on top of him being Que's brother, is the only reason I started fucking with this little nigga again. I wouldn't say I trusted him all the way, but he was family. Which means I'll always be there for my little nigga.

"Stepping away from the game, was it worth it?"

"I wouldn't be me if I said I didn't miss it. Being in the streets has been a part of me since I was a little nigga. It gave me a rush that I don't know how to explain. Yet, it wasn't worth Raven stressing about whether I'll come home or if I'll get locked up. She deserves better than the worry. As much as I do miss the shit, I'm man enough to say I love my woman more than the streets. I would miss her presence more than I will miss all this shit, so yea, it was worth it."

"I feel you. You still a part of it though by cleaning my money for me."

"Old habits are not easy to break," I told him.

He stayed for a minute and talked to me a while longer before leaving. Looking around my shop, I smiled, amazed at how far a nigga had come. After my mom was murdered by her best friend over my pops, I was heartbroken. A nigga became a demon and caused havoc in the streets. I'm just glad a nigga still have his freedom and life. That was another reason I had to give Raven the world. It was because of her a nigga was a changed man and can still say I wasn't in a grave or in a cell.

Thinking of Raven, I pulled out my phone and gave her a call. When she ain't answer, I decided to call Renz. It wasn't like her to ignore a nigga's phone call, so I wanted to make sure she was straight.

"What's good, nigga?" Renz picked up the phone.

"Ain't shit, how's fatherhood?"

"Shit would be great, but a nigga ain't been able to enjoy it how much I want to."

"What you mean?"

"That hoe ass Detective Robinson came into the hospital and touched my daughter and MIMI. The only thing I been focused on is getting at that hoe ass nigga."

"Say word? Fuck that nigga still lingering around for?"

"Bruh, I really think this nigga is obsessed with Niomi. Ain't no fucking other reason for this nigga to be around."

"So, what are you going to do? He's twelve, that's a whole different ball game."

"Shit, I know. I can't even find the nigga right now. I went down to the precinct he works at and they talking about the nigga took a leave of absence. I got one of the little homies looking for him, but honestly, I don't know how I'm going to handle the hoe ass nigga. I killed niggas for less, so he has to be dealt with. I just have no clue how I'm going to do it."

"Well shit, you know I'm down for whatever, nigga."

"My brother, what's up with you though? Nigga, how's that legal money treating you?"

"Shit, the same way it's treating you. Where Raven at though? I been calling her phone and she ain't answering."

"What do you mean? I haven't seen her all day."

"What, you just now getting home? She said she was going to see Niomi and the baby."

"I been here all day, she ain't swing through. You need me to ride with you to look for her?"

"I'ma swing by the house first, maybe she ended up falling asleep. I'll call you once I figure shit out."

"Alright, nigga, be safe."

"Always, you too." I hung up the phone with Renz and hopped straight into my black on black Benz. The shop was half an hour away from the crib, but I got there in fifteen minutes. Pulling into the driveway, I saw Raven's all-white Range Rover and that gave me a sense of relief. Heading in the crib I took the elevator up to the second floor and headed to our room. Raven was stretched out on our bed sleep with the kids right in front of her. I smiled at the sight in front of me before taking a picture of them. Grabbing Jr. first, I took him to their room and put him in his crib before doing the same thing with Raina.

"Ray, get up." I kissed her lips and she stirred in her sleep. Opening her eyes, she smiled at me.

"Hey, why are you home so early?"

"I couldn't reach you, so I got worried. Why didn't you go to see Niomi and the baby?"

"I wasn't feeling well, so I decided to stay in. Sorry to have you worry. Soon as I put the kids down, I went straight to sleep."

"You sure you straight?" I asked, looking at her skeptical, I couldn't put my finger on exactly what it was, but something was bothering Raven. I knew her too well.

"Yes, I'm fine. I love you, Demontae."

"I love you more. Lay back and rest, I'll take care of everything, dinner and the kids. You deserve a break."

"I love you. Thank you for being the prefect husband."

"Nah, thank you," I told her, heading out the room to start dinner. I knew it was something she wanted to talk to me about, but I figured she would talk to me about it when she's ready.

Chapter 10 Carmen

"What the fuck?" I said as I tried to urinate and felt a burning sensation. Looking in my underwear, I saw the discharge and knew something wasn't right. Hopping in the shower, I quickly showered and got dressed, then dressed Quincy.

"Ms. White, from the looks of it and what you describe as your symptoms, it appears you have Gonorrhea. I won't know exactly until your lab results come back, but I feel that's what it is. We will have to wait until the results to give you a shot. I'll prescribe you medication for bacterial infection to help with the burning and discharge. We'll have your results by tomorrow," my gynecologist said before she left the hospital room. I sat there perplexed at what she just told me.

"Ghonorrea?" I repeated out loud. I couldn't believe Raulin had cheated and brought a disease back to me. Hurt wasn't a strong enough word to describe how I was feeling.

After the Medical assistant came in and gave me discharge papers, I was free to go. Calling Raulin, I got his voicemail and that pissed me off more. Calling him again, the same thing happened, and I gave up. I was hurt and the only thing I wanted to do was go see my best friend, J'liyah.

Pulling up to her condo, I smiled at how my best bitch was living. She had a little boo named Davon and from what she told me, he was perfect. She was happy and I was happy for her. At least one of us was.

"Ayee, what it do, best bitch!" Jaliyah said, opening the door. She had her tongue out while she twerked. As bad as I wanted to twerk with her because it's been a minute since we'd seen one another, the mood that I was in wouldn't let me.

"What's wrong?" Jliyah asked, taking Quncity out my arms. She must have noticed the somber look on my face.

"Raulin cheated on me and gave me a disease."

"What?"

"Yes, and I feel so stupid I feel like I'm letting a man take me away from myself. Ever since Raulin came into my life, I feel like he's been taking more than he's been giving. I thought when Quincy was born, it would bring us closer together, but our son has really shown me the true Raulin. I mean, from jump he wasn't shit, and I knew it then. Then he made me fall in love and now I feel like he's taking advantage of the love I give him. He doesn't even want me to go back to school," I cried.

"Wipe your tears, Carmen, and remember who you are! You can't let him have that much control over you! Now I won't say leave him because that's your choice and only you can make it. I will say this, you're not living just for you anymore. You have a son. Go back to school, Carmen, and forget how Raul feels about it. I love you." She gave me a hug and I cried in her arms. I was thankful to have my bestie. She's always been the light during the dark times.

One in the morning, that's the time Raulin decided to step foot in our home. I shook my head and laughed as he walked in our room like nothing was wrong.

"What you still doing up?" He asked. I stood up and smack him in his face. He wrapped his hand around my neck, and I clawed at his eyes. I kept hitting him, making sure to get him good a couple of times in his face. I was full of range, and he was the cause of it.

"What the fuck is wrong with you, Carmen!" He barked, grabbing my hands.

"You dirty dick bastard, how could you just stand there like your dick is not burning, you sick fuck?!" I screamed, pulling my hands away from him.

As bad as I didn't want to cry, I couldn't help the tears that fell out my eyes. I hated the man standing in front of me. I hated him for giving me a disease. I hated him. I hated him for leaving me alone while I went through my postpartum depression. I hated him for all the hell he put me through when I first told him I was pregnant. I hated him for wanting me to sacrifice my dreams. I hated him for missing the birth of our son, and I hated him for cheating on me and giving me a disease.

"I don't know what you're talking about."

"So now you're going to play with my intelligence. I have a disease and I know it. I'll have my results tomorrow. I know something's not right with my pussy and you're the only person I've had sex with. How could you cheat on me, Raulin, after everything I sacrifice for you?!" I screamed.

"What do you mean, Carmen? How could I not? All you do is nag a nigga about the shit I was involved in before we started fucking around. You want a nigga to change, but this is who I am, and who I always been! You not making it easy for a nigga to love you."

"You know what, I'm done with this relationship! I'm leaving and I'm taking Quincy away from you!" I tried to walk by him, but he grabbed my arm.

"Carmen, you're not going nowhere and my son damn sure ain't. Don't test the nigga I am. I would hate to bring harm to the woman I love but threatening to take my seed will bring out the demon in me. Now look, I apologize for giving you a disease, and I'm man enough to admit that was fucked up. But every time we have a problem, you can't leave. We are going to work this shit out," he said and turned his back to me as he walked out the room.

I screamed from the depth of my soul because I was in a dark place. I was feeling trapped and I desperately wanted out.

***

"You sure you don't need my notes?" My classmate, Elijuan, asked as we left out of the class.

This was the last class of the day and I was thankful for it. I missed my son. I have been back in school for a week now after taking Jliyah's advice and it was hard getting used to being a mother and a student. Raulin had no idea I was back in school and I knew if he found out, he would have a fit. He tried his best to get me to talk to him, but I wouldn't. I was fed up with him, and now it was like we were getting worse. He barely came home and barely sees our baby. The depression was getting worse and I felt alone. I wanted to talk to Renz about everything that was going on, but he and Niomi were already doing a lot by keeping Quincy for me while I went to school when Ma, Raulin's mother, couldn't keep him. Renz and I had several talks about me coming clean to Raul, but I felt like I didn't have to. He didn't get that school was a part of me, I needed this to provide a future for my son. I wanted him to be proud of his mother. It was fuck Raul. I didn't care who felt like I was wrong keeping him in the dark about me returning to school. He wasn't around anyways, so it's no point of telling him something he would know if he was at home more.

"I'm sure. Thank you for being such a life saver and helping me with the things I don't understand. You have been such a huge help. It's been hard getting back in the flow of school with having a newborn at home.

"A newborn? It don't look like you had a kid."

"Yea, I did. I'll text you when I get home," I told Elijuan before hopping in my ride. The whole way from school to Renz's, I thought about if continuing this relationship with Raul is what I wanted. I love him, but I wasn't happy. If I wasn't happy, then what's the point?

Chapter 11 Detective Robinson

I slowly trailed behind Niomi and couldn't help but to get upset for having to waste my time stalking her. I don't know exactly what it was about her, but something had me intrigued. From the very first encounter at the bank, I wanted Niomi. At first it was harmless, nothing more than thinking she was a beautiful woman. My feelings eventually grew when she would call me afraid because the suspects that robbed the bank were still out there. The more she leaned on me out of fear, the more I began to catch feelings for her. When she called me the night she got hit by the car, I knew she found out exactly what I always knew. I figured once I arrested everyone involved, she would be grateful and come running to me.

Imagine the surprise I got when I went to check on her after handling another case found out she couldn't remember me, or anything else for that matter. That created more drive to get Renz and his crew arrested. I felt like they were taking advantage of Niomi and the fact that she couldn't remember what happened. I'd been trying to do everything in my power to make sure their asses got put in a cage, but I wasn't successful. The problem is there was no proof, just years of detective work and a hunch. That was the point of me talking to Rich Boy. I knew he had ties to Lorenzo and I was going to use him for my benefit.

The rest of the crew was an added bonus, but my plan was to get Lorenzo White out the way so Niomi can belong to me. I hated that I had to go through all of this to get her, but she worth it all. I was willing to put everything on the line to make her mine. I watched as she pulled into the doctor's office parking lot, stepped out the car and opened the back door. I parked right next to her, got out my car and crept up behind her. She turned around and jumped when she noticed it was me.

"What are you doing here?" She asked, holding onto her daughter tightly. I chuckled then stepped closer. Rubbing my hand on the side of her face, I smiled at her before moving a string of hair to the side. She was so beautiful.

"I came to see you, Niomi. I know you lost your memory so the events before you woke up from your coma are a little blurry, but I want to remind you."

"Remind me of what?" She asked, smacking my hand away. I giggled because this feisty was turning me on.

She thought she was scaring me away when she was just making me more infatuated with her.

"Remind you of how scared you were. You were afraid they would come back to finish the job. Remind you of how it felt when they held a gun to your face when the bank got robbed!" I didn't mean raise and get belligerent with her, but it was pissing me off how she could be married to the man who caused her so much pain.

"Okay, I don't remember that. I'm glad I don't remember a traumatic experience like that. What does that have to do with the reason you're stalking me!" She yelled. Her daughter started crying and she rocked her. I watched as she looked around and I stepped closer.

"We both know you're married to the man who, he along with his crew, caused you traumatic experience."

"I have no idea what you're talking about."

"Yes, you do, and it's just a matter of time before justice is served," I told her, walking away from her and heading towards my ride.

"What do you mean by that?" I heard her yell. Chuckling, I just drove off.

Taking out my phone, I called Rich Boy. I was becoming more irate the longer these niggas were free and not behind bars.

"Yea?" He answered

"You got that info yet?"

"Nah, I'm still working on it."

"You must don't want your freedom because it seems to me like you're not working hard enough for it. You have one week," I said, hanging up on him. Hitting the steering wheel repeatedly, I freaked out as I thought about Niomi spending another week with Renz. I hated to admit it, but it was driving me crazy not being the one she came home too.

Chapter 12 Raul

Beating on Diamond's door, I waited impatiently for her to answer. It was fucked up Diamond gave me a disease. On top of that, my ass gave it to Carmen and that shit just added more problems to the problems we were already having.

"Why the fuck you banging on my door like that, Raulin?" She opened the door and I wrapped my hands around her neck, leading us in her crib. She tried to scratch my hand, but that wasn't doing shit. Letting her ass go after noticing her eyes watering, I had to tuck my hands in my jeans pocket so I wouldn't catch a domestic violence case.

"Bitch, your dirty pussy ass gave me a disease."

"Look, Raulin, I didn't know I had a disease until after we had sex. If I would have known, I wouldn't have had sex with you."

"You expect me to believe your pussy burning and you didn't know?"

"I wasn't having symptoms until the day after we had sex. I'm sorry, don't be mad at me, Raul. Please forgive me."

"Bitch, forgive you? I brought a disease back home to my bitch. There's no forgiving that shit."

"Well nobody told you to fuck your bitch after you fuck me. You can't care about her too much. If you did, your ass wouldn't been fucking me."

"Bitch, what you say?" I asked, stepping closer to her and she stepped back.

"Get out, or I will call the police!" She screamed.

"Call the police? You a rat ass bitch now, Diamond?"

"Just get out."

"Watch your back. I'ma have some bitches in the hood do your trifling ass dirty," I told her and headed out.

At one point in time, I had nothing but love for Diamond. I thought she was my best friend, but now I see first-hand how grimy the bitch was. Leaving out of her shit, I called one of the home girls from the hood and put a price on that bitch head. She wouldn't get away with giving me a disease. Hopping in my ride, I headed in the direction of my trap. The main trap that made the most money. When I pulled up, I saw Rich Boy hopping out his ride.

"Fuck you doing here?" I barked, walking up to him. This was the second time this nigga came and I wasn't sure why, but that shit raised red flags like a motherfucker. I wasn't fucking with the nigga and I damn sure wouldn't sell him no product, so there was no point of him lingering around.

"Damn, that's the type of energy you bring when it's your first time seeing your boy in a minute?"

"I don't fuck with you, nigga, so what's the real reason you here?"

"I'm just thinking about that time we robbed the bank. I feel like I didn't get paid as much as I should of from you and them niggas Diggy and Renz. I feel like I'm owed more money."

"Nigga, you had to have fucking falled and hit your head or some shit. I don't have no fucking clue about no bank jobs and no idea what niggas you speaking on."

"You know exactly who I'm speaking on, nigga, you fucking his sister. And you know exactly what bank Job I'm talking about. I'm owed more fucking money, so have that shit, or you ain't gon' like the nigga I'm turning into."

"You threatening a nigga?" I asked ,stepping closer to him. Rich Boy knew the kind of nigga I am and him threatening me wasn't sitting to well with me.

"Nah, just letting you know shit can get real fast." He chuckled, putting his hand up in a surrender motion, chuckling then heading back to his car. I wanted to take my glock out of my pocket and kill that nigga, but something was telling me not to. I watched the nigga drive off before I headed into the spot. As always, my niggas was getting to the money. After the fein that was in the trap when I walked in left out the door, I began to talk.

"I'm closing down this spot, shit ain't safe. Bag the product and money up, put it in the book bags and place them in my ride!" I barked. They didn't ask no questions but did as I asked. I wasn't sure where the fuck I was about to make the new at, but I wasn't comfortable with keeping shit the same after Rich Boy coming around twice. I didn't trust shit. And the fact this nigga brought up Renz, Diggy and the bank job wasn't sitting well with me. My gut was telling me Rich Boy was on some snake shit. One thing about me, I always listened to my gut.

Once we loaded the bags in my whip, I split up the guys and had them go help out with the other two traps before I headed home. A nigga was paranoid as hell riding around with all this white girl in my truck. When I got to the crib safely, a nigga felt a little better. Still, I had a huge problem. I had nowhere to store all this work. I couldn't store it at any of my other traps because it was already full of product. I had a storage unit more work stashed there, but that was at least two hours out of the city. If I were to make that trip tonight, I wouldn't get back late. That would have been the smart route, but I was trying to come back home at a decent hour and make shit right with Carmen. I could feel the hate she had for me whenever I was in her presence, and I didn't blame her. I been slacking and that's why I was trying to do better.

Walking in the crib with the book bags, I was met with Carmen coming down the stairs carrying Quincy. Looking at the suitcases by the door, I gave her a blank stare. It didn't take a fucking math genius to put two and two together. I wanted to strangle her ass but instead, I sat down, patiently waiting for her ass to tell me what the fuck she thought she was doing.

"You trying to leave a nigga?" I questioned when she didn't say shit. My voice was barely audible. It hurt to even say that shit. Carmen and Quincy were my whole world and it hurt to even think about coming home to this big ass crib without them.

"What's in the book bag, Raulin?" Carmen asked, avoiding my question.

"The book bag? You worried about these fucking book bags?"

"Yea, I am! I'm not stupid. I know what you do, and I know what that is. That's why I'm leaving! You put the street shit before us all the time! I'm done, Raulin."

"You done? You just gon' walk away and take my son? I love the fuck out of y'all, Carmen!"

"You love us? You put us in danger by bringing narcotics in our home? A home where I lay my head, a home where our son lay his head! You selfish bastard, how

93

could you?" The tears were running down her face. Quincy started to cry and I tried to grab him, but she moved out the way.

"Carmen, don't fucking do this! Damn, okay. I wanted to do better, so I decided to come home. I was going to put them in my office tonight and take it to the spot first thing in the morning."

"I need time, Raulin!"

"Time? Take all the time you need to get your head together but do it here! This house is big enough for us to be in together and never see each other."

"Move, Raulin!" She tried to walk pass me and I grabbed her free arm she wasn't using to hold my son.

"Let me go, Raul!" She screamed and a moment later, Renz was coming through the door. I wasn't sure where his ass came from because I didn't see his car in the driveway when I first pulled up.

"The fuck you just barging in my house for, nigga?" I asked, tossing the one book bag I still had on my shoulder onto the floor.

"Little nigga, get that base out your voice. I don't give a fuck whose home it is, when baby sis call, I come running."

"Fuck you want to do then, nigga? This my fucking family, know your place."

"What, nigga?" Renz asked, stepping up. Before I could say or do anything, Carmen was in the middle of us.

"Stop! This not what I want. I'll be at my brother's, Raulin, and that's final."

I watched as they walked out the door and a nigga didn't know what to do. Shit was fucked up. They said shit happened in threes. After losing my trap and my family on the same day, I couldn't help but wonder what fucked up shit would happen next.

Chapter 13 Raven

Logan had been calling me nonstop and I was getting irritated with him. I had to block him on Facebook and his phone number. He have been calling me private, and I was starting to realize he would be a problem.

"Who the fuck blowing you up like that?" Diggy looked at me with questioning eyes. This was the time I should have come clean and told Diggy about Logan, but I couldn't bring myself to tell him the truth. The kids and I were his world, and he knew nothing about Logan. Me allowing him to be around Jr would break his heart and I couldn't see me doing that.

"Bill collectors."

"When we start lying to each other?"

"Huh?" I asked, completely caught off guard by his question.

"When the fuck did bill collectors start calling private?"

Not able to come up with a quick enough response, I started stuttering and that caused his hand to go around my neck.

"You think I'm stupid? You fucking off? I'll kill you before I'll let you be with another nigga!" He gritted.

My eyes watered and I clawed at his hands because it was hard for me to breathe. He looked in my eyes and a few seconds later, let me go. I coughed profusely as I tried to catch my breath. I glared at him, a little hurt he would think I would step out on our marriage.

Before I could speak, he was out the room, and I was calling out after him.

"Diggy!" I called after him. Hearing the front door slam shut, I knew he was out the house.

At the sound of my phone ringing again, I decided to answer it.

"What!?" I screamed into the phone.

"Looks like trouble in paradise." I cringed at the sound of Logan's voice.

"What are you talking about?" I stuttered into the phone.

Hearing the front door open, I dropped my phone on the bed and ran to the door, thinking maybe Diggy was coming back. When I saw Logan at the bottom of the stairs, my heart dropped. Heading to my bedroom, I ran to my phone and dialed 911. Before I could tell the operator exactly what was going on, my hair grabbed from behind. Before I could scream or yell, I felt a sharp pain in my side.

"Ahhhh!" I yelled in agony.

The pain came again before he dropped me on the floor. I watch as he walked down the hall and seconds later, I could hear the kids crying. I tried to crawl, but I was bleeding too bad. I saw Jr. in his hands and cried as Logan look at me and smiled.

"I know your punk ass husband killed my sister. If you survive, tell him I'll be coming for him next."

I watched as he held Jr. in his arms. I tried to reach for him, but I could barely move, my eyes were becoming heavy. I could hear Raina still crying and as bad as I wanted to go after her, I couldn't.

"Hold on, baby," I said before everything went black.

***

"Raven, what happened?" Is the first thing I heard when I came to. blinking my eyes a few times to get adjusted to the light, I came face to face with Diggy's red eyes. I could tell he was crying and it was a painful sight to see. Diggy was very egotistical, him crying was something he never did.

Images of Logan taking Jr came to my mind and I cried.

"Logan."

"Who the fuck is Logan?" I could see the anger on Diggy's face and knew what I was about to say would only make him angrier. I had to come clean though, Jr's life was on the line.

"He's Laura's brother."

"Her brother? How the fuck that nigga know where we lay our heads? Shit's not adding up to me." Diggy said. He stood and paced the hospital floors back and forth. I could tell he was in deep thought, and I knew he wasn't expecting me to play a hand in it.

"I let him see Logan a few times. We met up at the park and he probably followed me home a few times. He came to me saying Laura was his only family and I felt bad, so I thought it would be okay to let him see Jr."

Soon as the words left my mouth, Diggy stopped pacing back and forth.

"What did you just say to me?" He turned around and look at me, his light face turning red. "You let a motherfuckin' stranger see my damn seed, he nigga follows you home, stabbed you twice, leaving you for dead, and took my fucking son! All because you thought it would be okay to let the nigga see my motherfucking son! That's my son, you had no fucking right!" By this time, he was yelling and I felt offended.

"YOUR SON? Was he your son when I was up in the middle of the night changing not only *our* daughter's diaper, but his as well?! Was he just your son when I fed, clothed and bathed him?! ME! I did that, NOT YOU!"

The nurse came in and asked us to calm down. Once she was gone, Diggy and I stared at each other. Neither of us saying anything, we just breathed heavy. My side was hurting, but my heart was hurting more. My son was in the hands of a monster and I was responsible for it. Diggy left my hospital room without saying anything to me. I cried as I watched him walk away. Deep down in my heart, I knew we would never be the same.

Chapter 14 Carmen

Elijuan was the perfect distraction. He has been exactly what I needed to get my mind off Raulin. He became a great friend and I would be lying if I said I didn't have a small crush on him. Glancing over at him as we sat at the Starbuck's restaurant table studying, I couldn't help but to admire his features. His brown skin was perfect, and the full beard and nice line only attracted me more.

"You going to stare at me all day or are we going to get back to studying?" He asked, looking up from his book.

"Who said I was staring at you?" I asked with a smile.

"I could feel you were."

"Well, you're just that handsome to me."

"And you're beautiful to me, so what's next?"

"What do you mean what's next?"

"Shit, it's obvious I'm feeling you and you're feeling me too. Let's make this shit official."

"I'm not sure that's a good idea."

"Why not, because of your baby father?"

"Yea, he's not going to take me moving on too kindly."

"So, you're just going to let that nigga stop you from being happy?" He asked.

Not able to respond to his question, I decided to change the subject. There wasn't really much else to say. It had been two weeks since I walked out on Raulin, and I would be lying if I said I didn't miss him. He was blowing me up constantly but lately, he was giving me the space I needed. I was thankful for that. He was coming by to see Quincy, but we still haven't sat down to talk about me returning home. Honestly speaking, I wasn't sure if I wanted to go back home.

"You want to come over? I really been enjoying your company?" I asked Elijuan as we left Starbuck's.

"You sure your brother would be straight with that?"

"Yea, why not? I'm grown and I live there too."

He didn't say anything else and I was thankful for that.

***

"Wake up, shorty, someone's at the door," Elijuan said, nudging me.

Looking around, I noticed we were on the couch. We stayed up until the wee hours of the morning, talking about everything. I don't even remember me falling asleep. All I remember was not wanting Elijuan to leave because I was enjoying his company.

"Damn, who can be here this early?" I asked, looking at my phone.

It was nine in the morning and I wasn't sure who would be stopping by this early. Elijuan and I had fallen asleep on the couch, and I was a little nervous about my brother seeing him. Not because he would say something, but I was sure I would receive a lecture from him. I could hear him now. *"Carmen, so that means you and Raul are done, right? Don't play with another man's feelings because you're unsure of yours."* He would say that and so much more.

"Coming," I called out before opening the door. I almost shitted on myself when I saw Raulin on the other side of the door with Quincy.

"What are you doing here? You're supposed to keep Quincy all weekend."

"Some shit came up and I have to go take care of it." Raulin bypassed me. As he placed the car seat Quincy was in on the ground, he saw Elijuan. "Who the fuck are you?" He barked.

Elijuan looked at me and didn't say shit. He just stood up as he stared at Raul. The tension was so thick in here, not even a damn machete could cut through it.

"What, this nigga can't here or some shit? Who the fuck is this nigga, Carmen?" Raulin ask, walking over to Elijuan.

Elijuan chuckled before running one of his hands over his waves.

"Look, he's my classmate."

"Classmate? Fuck you talking about, Carmen?" He barked, moving closer to me.

Elijuan stepped closer and Raulin looked at him.

"Fuck you step closer for, nigga?"

Elijuan gave a cocky laugh and then looked at me.

"Out of respect for you, your child and your brother's home, I'm going to leave. See you in class," he said. He walked pass Raul and they stared each other down before he walked out of the door. Raulin looked at me for a good five minutes without saying anything.

"You think a nigga stupid, Carmen?"

"What are you talking about now?" I asked, bending down so I could be eye level with Quincy's car seat. Kissing my baby boy a few times on the cheek, I stood up to face Raulin.

"I'm talking about how a nigga didn't even know your ass was back in school. On top of that, it's early as fuck in the morning, and I come over here to you and a nigga in your brother's crib. Ain't no motherfucking nigga coming all the way to the suburbs first thing in the morning. You look like you just woke up, so that nigga spent the night. Keep that shit one hunnit, you fucked the nigga?"

"You fucked another bitch, didn't you?"

"You want to fucking play with me, Carmen?" Raulin asked, stepping closer to me, I could look in his eyes and see he wasn't bullshitting. To avoid unnecessary drama, I decided to tell the truth and put his mind to ease.

"Look, he's just a classmate. After studying, we came over here and stayed up all night talking. We fell asleep and woke up when you knocked on the door. "

"Talk? You expect for me to think that you just talked to a nigga?" Raul walked up on me, backing me into the wall. Wrapping his hand around my throat, I could see the anger in his eyes.

Looking down at our son, water filled the rim of my eyes as I thought about him having to see this. Regardless if he understood what was going on or not, it was heartbreaking to know he was watching the toxicity tht his father and I shared. I tried to claw at Raulin's hands as I saw Niomi and Renz coming down the stairs. Niomi had this horrific expression on her face. Renz was following behind Niomi with his head down. When he looked up, his eyes came into contact with mine. Raulin, who had his back to them, had no idea they were behind him. Before I could blink, Renz had Raulin in the air, then slammed him. Niomi rushed to tend to me while Renz and Raul went at it. I wasn't sure how Raul hopped up so fast, but they were standing in the living room throwing punches. I was surprised to see how good Raul was able to hold his own against my brother. Still he was no match for Renz. My son was crying at the top of his lungs from all the commotion. The last thing I wanted to do was see the man I love and my big brother going at it like two enemies in the streets.

"Stop! Stop!" I yelled, grabbing Renz. Raul threw another punch and it barely hit me. If Renz hadn't pushed me slightly, I'm sure Raul would have hit me.

"Raulin, get the fuck out! You have my damn son scared out of his mind all because of your insecurities," I said, picking up Quincy.

"Fuck your hoe ass," Raulin said and Renz stepped closer.

"Nigga, what?"

"Let him go," I said.

Raulin stared at me for a moment, nodded his head and let out a cocky laugh before walking pass me then out the door. I looked at Niomi and Renz, embarrassed. Before I could apologize, the sound of my niece 'scries filled the air.

"I'll get her," Niomi said before heading back up the stairs.

"Look, Renz, I apologize for bringing all this drama in your home."

"Carmen, you know I love you, but you have to get your shit together. This wasn't the life I envisioned for you. If you want to be with Raulin, you have to figure the shit out and make it work. If not, you have to let the nigga go or the shit is just going to get worse." He gave me a kiss on the cheek before he headed upstairs.

I could see he was disappointed in me and that hurt me. It seemed like I'd been doing that more and more lately. Wiping away the tears that fell, I got my son and his car seat and headed to my room. I hated Raulin and the more I thought about it, I began to feel like it was best for us to end our relationship.

Still Caught Up With A Trap God

Chapter 15 Detective Robinson

"Welcome back, how was the vacation?" Wordy, one of the many detectives that worked at the same precinct as me, asked.

"It was cool," I said, taking a seat at my desk.

Opening my desk drawer, I glanced at the printed picture I took of Niomi's Facebook. She was so beautiful. I took six weeks off just so I would be able to take down her husband and his friends. To know I wasn't successful stressed me a bit. These damn criminals were able to break the law and not get caught, but I disgruntled with the situation. Rich boy went ghost and I felt dumb for giving him as much time as I did. Good thing for me, I'd been watching him for weeks before I pulled him over that day. He wasn't the most intelligent criminal and that's why he was my choice of person to get to turn. I knew he would be easy to turn because he moved recklessly.

I had all kinds of pictures of him with drugs and flexing money on the internet. He was the kind of man who loved to be conspicuous and that would be his downfall. The only problem is now I had to spend time locating him.

I worked twelve hours a day and the time I needed to look for him would be on my personal time. Niomi was worth it though.

Opening the drawer again to pull out the file I had on Rich Boy, I came into the contact with the pill bottle that held my medication. Manic I Bipolar Disorder was the correct terminology for my diagnosis. Depakote was the medication he gave me but I never took the pills. I wasn't damn bipolar. I don't care how many people said I was and needed the medication, I wasn't going to take them. The only reason I had the pills in my desk was or just in case purposes. Just in case I was in a situation where my anger got the best of me. At times, I did get irate as fuck. That, I could admit. Putting the pill bottle in my pocket, I took out my burner cell and called RichBoy, only to meet his voicemail. Shaking my head, I put the phone back in my pocket. Getting up from the desk, I headed to the restroom area. My sergeant's voice at the front desk caught my attention by saying my name.

"Detective Robinson?" She said.

Looking her way, I noticed she was looking straight ahead at Niomi. I rushed into the bathroom and began pacing back and forth. I forgot I told her which damn precinct I worked at. The plan was spiraling out of control and I was starting to freak out. Taking my hands, I began to box the air. At this moment, this was the only thing I could do. I wanted to hit a wall or punch a few mirrors, but I couldn't because I was at work. I took my frustrations out by punching the air until I wore myself out. I wasn't sure what Niomi was out there telling her, but I would deny it because good thing she didn't have any proof.

When making my moves, I was very inconspicuous and articulate. Niomi thought she was coming to my boss with some hardcore evidence, but she wasn't. Once I told myself there was no proof, I walked out of the bathroom. As soon as I was about to sit at my desk, my sergeant called me to her office.

"Everything okay, Sarge?" I asked, taking a seat.

She sat behind her desk, folded her hands and let out a deep breath.

"Look, I'm just going to come out and say it. The news that I have, the complaint, is very disturbing and I would hope that there's no truth to it. Are you stalking Niomi White?"

"Stalking?" I asked, leaning forward as if I couldn't hear her the first time.

"Yes, she's making some very disturbing accusations."

"Sarge, I only know Mrs. White from the bank robbery where I worked. I went to keep her updated about the case, but she had suffered brain trauma and couldn't remember the case. That was my last time seeing her."

"Alright, Detective Robinson, I believe you. How was your vacation?"

"It was okay. Am I free to go now?" I asked, and she nodded her head yes.

Niomi coming up to me didn't do anything to deter my mission from making her mines. In all honesty, she just motivated me more.

Chapter 16 Raul

" *A* lot of guns, money, drugs put in kitchen cabinets, tryna rob who the guys they ain't really having it ."* I rapped along to the lyrics of Biyaa Spazz as I sat behind the steering wheel in my cocaine white Benz. I only pulled out this whip on special occasions and this was a fucking special occasion. Today was my big brother's birthday and I was having a block party right in the hood for my nigga. I was going to celebrate and turn the hood up like he would. I missed my nigga every day. We were a few years apart, but we were close. It put me in a dark place when I lost him.

Stepping out the ride, my black and white Dior shoes hit the pavement. It was a nice day so the all-white jeans I wore and the button up Dior shirt had these bitches' eyes all on me. These bitches could smell the money. Sitting on the hood of my whip with my bottle of Henny in my hand, I took a sip as I checked out the scenery. Everyone was out showing love. Niggas approached me and dapped me up while bitches stood off to the side trying to get my attention.

"Happy birthday, nigga. I miss you," I said out loud before pouring some Hennessy on the floor for my brother. I watched as Diggy and Renz approached me. I stood up because I wasn't sure what them niggas were on. I hadn't talked to Renz since we fought at his home weeks ago.

"What's good, nigga?" Renz said and I nodded.

"You still tripping off that fight?" Diggy asked, dapping me up.

"Nah, I just don't know the energy niggas on."

"Look, nigga. At the end of the day, that's my baby sister. I stay out y'all shit 'cause that's y'all shit. As far as you putting your hands on her, that's some shit I should have bodied your ass for. Instead, I gave you an ass whooping so be happy with that."

"Yea, alright, nigga. I respect that shit . I wasn't right putting my hands on her, I just couldn't take it when I saw that nigga there." I shook my head after saying the words 'cause the thought alone had a nigga's trigger finger itching. I love Carmen and my son, and I wasn't going to allow another nigga to come in and take what's mine that shit was dead. I'd been giving Carmen space and grinding hard in the streets, but I couldn't shake the feeling that something bad was about to happen. That just prompted me want to make amends and get my family back. I knew Carmen wasn't ready, so I just played the back field.

"She need to hear that, nigga, not I," Renz said.

Before I could respond, Diamond's ass was approaching.

"Can we talk?" This bitch had the nerve to ask. I looked at this bitch like she was stupid.

Looking over at the group of bitches giving us lustful stares, I waved for them to come over.

"What's up, Diggy, Renz and Raul?" Tanisha asked, coming up to us. She was a girl from around the hood.. She gave us a quick hug and bypassed Diamond, who was staring with a mug on her face.

"Ain't shit. You trying make a band?" I asked her and her shiny ass lips turned into a huge smile.

"For sure, how?"

"Beat this bitch up." I looked at Diamond.

"I'm pregnant with your baby!" Diamond blurted out and Tanisha looked at me skeptically. I didn't believe shit this bitch was saying.

"Man, this bitch lying, beat her ass," I said to Tanisha.

She turned to Diamond and Diamond squared up. I knew Diamond had hands, but I saw the way Tanisha got down and nobody was fucking with her. Tanisha put her hands up and a crowd formed around them. Diamond threw two punches and it connected to Tanisha. Tanisha smiled before she ran up on her. Diamond went for her hair and got a good grip on it. Tanisha started throwing mean ups and you can tell them hits were affecting Diamond. Diamond still wouldn't let go of Tanisha's hair, but that ain't mean shit, she was fucking her up. I looked at her homegirls as they started moving forward. Before I knew it, they were all in the fight and Diamond was on the ground getting stomped out.

"Alright ,y'all stop this shit," Renz said as he and Diggy broke that shit up. I stayed in the back and watched the shit unfold. I ain't give a fuck about this rat ass bitch Diamond.

As Renz helped her to her feet, I could see the blood coming from Diamond's face and that shit made a nigga smile. Once she was on her feet, she snatched away from Renz then looked at me.

"This ain't over, nigga. I know too much about you!" She barked and I pulled out my strap.

"Say what, bitch? You threatening a nigga?" I pointed my gun in her direction. I wasn't too worried about anyone calling twelve. This was my neighborhood. I wasn't just a nigga who grew up in this neighborhood. I was a nigga who got rich and provided for the neighborhood. I paid bills for people, brought little niggas in the hood shoes, gave little girls money and even bought groceries. I could have done more, but a nigga did a lot for the hood and that's why my people fuck with me.

"You wildin'," Diggy said. He moved the gun out her face then looked at her. "Take your ass on for this psychotic ass nigga murder your ass." She must've known his words held truth to them 'cause the bitch got on.

"Nigga, you still hot headed as fuck," Diggy said as I sat back on the hood of my car.

"Shit, that bitch crossed the line. What's up with you though, any news on that fuck nigga who took your seed?" I asked him. I could feel the anger radiating from his body.

"Hell nah, not yet. I'm going to find that nigga and when I do, it's bad for that nigga."

"I feel you, nigga. Let me know if you need some shit from me," I told him and he nodded.

All three of us passed a blunt back and forth while I took in the scenery. I thought my eyes were playing tricks on me. Walking over to this nigga Fatts that stayed in the hood, he tried to dap me up, but I left the nigga hanging there.

"Who this nigga? I ain't never seen him in the neighborhood and I know he ain't fuck with Que 'cause I never seen the nigga in the hood before."

"What's the real reason you mad at me about? Is it the fact you lost your family, nigga?" He said and I chuckled. Laughing, I punched his ass in his face and we started going blow for blows.

I could hear Fatts saying for us to cut it out, but a nigga ain't give a fuck. I was emotional and this nigga speaking on me losing my family meant Carmen confided in him.

"Man, fuck is y'all niggas doing?"

Renz and Diggy rushed over to where I was to break up the fight. I pushed Renz off me and the first set of eyes I came in contact with were Carmen's. I looked at her, ready to take my anger out her. She betrayed what we had when she took it to another nigga and decided to tell him what the fuck we had going on. On top of that, this nigga just kept popping up, so to me, the situation between them was a lot deeper than Carmen led on. Walking up to her, she stepped back and Renz grabbed me.

"Nigga, watch how you handle this shit with my sister. Don't let outsiders know what the fuck y'all got going on, and don't let what happened at the house repeat itself. Keep your hands to yourself, little nigga," Renz said.

I ain't say shit back to him, wasn't much to say. The person I needed to talk to was Carmen. I wasn't with the games she was playing. If she wanted to fuck with that nigga, I would let her. Honestly speaking, I was tired of this love shit. I was tired of letting another motherfucker have so much control over me. I was acting like a bitch fighting over her when it was obvious to me, she wanted that nigga.

"Meet me at home," I said before I hopped in my ride and sped off.

Chapter 17 Carmen

When Jliyah invited me to Que's block party, I was against it. After my bestie convinced me to come, I asked Niomi to watch my baby and she agreed to it. Imagine my surprise when we arrived and it was a lot of people circling around a big altercation. When I noticed who was fighting, I couldn't believe my eyes. I wasn't even sure how Elijuan even got invited or how he knew about the party.

"Your baby dad wild, you look, beautiful." Elijuan stepped up as if he was going to hug me, and I stepped back. I wasn't sure what he thought, but he was delusional if he thought after he fought Raul I would be hugging on him. Yes, he was a friend and one I considered to be good, but he just fought my child's father in public.

"What are you even doing here?" I asked him.

"Shit, my cousin from the neighborhood, he invited me. I ain't know this was your baby dad's people or that you would even be here," he said and I shook my head.

I really didn't have any words for him at this moment. I needed to get home to the house that I shared with Raulin. The look in his eyes let me know he wasn't playing with me. Turning to Jliyah, I ignored Elijuan and asked for her to take me home since she was my ride here.

***

I could smell smoke as soon as I walked in the door. I shook my head because Raulin knew how I felt about smoke being in the house. Hearing music, I headed to the back of the house where his office was. Opening the door, he had a blunt in his hand with a glass cup in the other. The Hennessy bottle was on his desk, so I figure that was what he was drinking.

His eyes were red and low and the way he looked at me made me fa little uncomfortable. I could see the anger dancing around in his eyes as if his eyes were a stage and the anger was a ballet dancer.

"Are you going to sit down?" He finally asked after the pregnant pause. He sipped his drink, set it on the table and waved me over. He nodded to the seat in front of his desk and I took a seat.

"Look, I know what this looks like, but I swear-" That's all I was able to get out before he started chuckling and shaking his head.

"Carmen, you take me for some clown ass nigga? You don't even fuck with parties or that type of scenery. It's a coincidence I see you and that nigga at my brothers' block party? You going to disrespect me like that?" He swiped his hand and knocked the glass off the table, causing me to jump.

"I swear, Raulin, I didn't know he would be there. I was just as surprised to see him. Look, I'd never disrespect you like that."

"But you would disrespect me to the point of fucking with another nigga. You know this my city, I got the city on lock. You thought word wouldn't travel back to me?"

"I didn't move on. It's funny how you questioning me when you were the one cheating on me and brought me back a disease. You didn't even give a fuck! I was breastfeeding our child, what if it was some serious shit?" My doctor had called me the next day after I left the hospital to confirm indeed it was what we thought. I was so embarrassed when I had to go back in there to get a shot.

"You're right, and I'm man enough to apologize for that shit. That was me being reckless, I can only apologize so many times though. I'm tired of this break shit ,so tell me what you want to do."

"Look, I need more time."

"Say less, I'm tired of waiting." He got up and left me there looking and feeling stupid.

After a few minutes of waiting, thinking he was going to come back, I got up and headed to the front of the house. I shook my head because the house was a mess. Heading upstairs, I walked in the bedroom. Raul was sitting on the bed with his back to me. I ignored him, grabbed me some silk pajamas and headed to the shower. Getting in, I let the hot water run over my skin as I stood there in deep thought. I wasn't sure what I wanted to do about Raulin and I's relationship. So many changes would have to be made before we could be back together, but I'd be lying if I said I didn't miss our home and him. After I got out the shower, I headed downstairs and began cleaning. Once the kitchen was done, I took out food to cook. I was so in my zone with the music playing and cooking, I didn't realize Raulin was in the kitchen until he spoke.

"What, you spending a night?"

"A night? This my home, I live here."

"Shit, I can't tell. What you cooking?"

"Lasagna."

"My favorite."

"Yea, with all the fast food bags laying around, I'm sure you can eat a home cooked meal." He sat down and nodded his head.

"So, how's school?"

"It's great. I love my professors, the work is easy, and I'm excited."

"That's good."

"How are things with you?"

"Shit, you know I lost my family, so I'm doing as expected."

"And what about the other stuff?"

"It doesn't matter, you claim that part of my life is the reason you're not here. Why you asking about the shit?" He looked at me skeptically. This was one of the turns off I had with Raulin, he's always so paranoid. He feels like everyone is out to get him.

"Calm down, I'm just asking, you know I'm always here to talk."

"You were never interested in my lifestyle."

"Is that the reason why?"

"The reason why what?" He stared in my eyes and I turned away to look in the oven and check on the lasagna. I love this man so much, it was too much to bare at times.

"The reason you cheated? Was she listening when I wasn't?"

"Come on, Carmen, don't start this shit."

"Why not? I want to know. Why did you risk everything we have!"

"Look, you were stressing a nigga and she was there to vent to. We were talking, then we fucked and that was that."

"That was that." I chuckled, shaking my head; this nigga is unbelievable.

"Look, I made a mistake but I'm done begging for another chance. Tomorrow, I'll go find me a crib."

"You're letting me keep the house?"

"Why wouldn't I? You're my child's mother and you have my son, I don't need this big ass crib anyways."

The thought of us really breaking up caused my heart to ache. I hated that we were coming to this, but this is where we were. The only way our relationship would last is if I accepted what he does, or if he left the streets alone. And I didn't see neither one happening.

Chapter 18 Diggy

"Are you hungry?" Raven asked, coming into the guest bedroom that has been my room for the last couple of weeks. I didn't trust I wouldn't strangle her ass while lying next to her every night. My son was still missing and that was on her.

"Nah, I'm straight," I told her as I continued to get dressed. I had word that Laura's best friend, Kemani, was back in town. I was about to get up with her to see what all she knew about Laura's hoe ass brother. I know she wouldn't give up the information willingly, but that was fine because I was going to force the shit out of her with my gun.

"How long are you going to go without speaking to me?" She asked, turning around. I could see her holding her side where she was stabbed. The cut healed, but it had her moving a lot slower. That was another reason for me to kill that hoe ass nigga. As much as I put the blame on Raven for the part she played, I blamed myself ten times more. I was so livid the day my son was kidnapped, I didn't close back the gate. That's the only reason that nigga was able to access my home. I fucked up and that nigga took my seed and almost killed my wife.

"Look, I'll be back later, don't wait up." I kissed her on the cheek and walked pass her. We no doubt had shit to discuss, but I wasn't discussing shit until my son was back. The time I would be using to have the conversation with Raven was time spent away from making sure my son was straight.

***

Pulling up to Kemani's house, I dapped up one of my niggas, B-Moore.

"She's still in the house, she hasn't come out yet," he told me, and I nodded my head.

One thing about being a nigga of my caliber, I was still respected in the streets. It wasn't shit to get people to handle my situations for me. Like B-Moore, I had him sitting on this bitch house all night.

"Good looking, wait for me out here." I dapped him up and walked up the steps. Covering the peephole, I knocked on the door and waited.

"Who is it?" Her ghetto ass called out. I didn't say shit, I just waited for her ass to open up the door. Quickly glancing around, I noticed nobody was out and that made me feel better about the body I was about to catch.

"Logan, you're early…" she began to say but stopped when she came face to face with me.

"Diggy, how did you… How did you find me?" She stuttered over her words as she walked backwards. Walking into her home, I closed the door.

"What, you thought leaving the city for a few months and then moving to this decent ass neighborhood was going to keep you off my radar? You just mentioned that nigga Logan, so I know your ass been in contact with him. And I'm sure you know about him kidnapping my son." I took out my gun and aimed it at her head. I was ready to off this bitch. Seeing the piss run down her leg, I shook my head. This bitch was scared shitless, but honestly speaking, I didn't give a fuck.

"Diggy, what did you expect from him? You killed his sister, we know you did. He's all we have left of her."

"Bitch, sit down!" I smacked her with the gun and she started to bleed. She held her head as she cried out, but a nigga ain't give a fuck. They should have taken what happened to Laura as a warning. I wasn't the nigga to fuck with and they were about to learn that the hard fucking way. Getting comfortable on the couch, I laid back and patiently waited for the nigga Logan to come. I was going to beat him until the nigga gave me the whereabouts of my son. Then I was going to kill both they asses and burn the damn house down with them in it. They didn't understand the side of me they woke up by coming after my family.

The knocking on the door caused Kemani to jump slightly. I already had her wipe the blood off her face for when that nigga Logan showed. Standing up, I nodded for her to follow me. I walked behind the door as I told her to open it. Pointing my gun at her, she nervously looked at me then opened the door.

"Logan, you brought the baby?" She asked and that made my heart smile. As soon as she said that, my son laughing could be heard and Logan was coming in the door.

"Put my son down, hoe ass nigga!" I barked, glancing behind him.

He look at me before I pressed the glock on the back of his head. He put the car seat down and as soon as he did, I beat him with my gun. He fell on the ground, and I didn't let up. I could feel the blood that splattered against my face and the bones that broke as I hit him, and I still didn't let up. It wasn't until Kemani tried to run that I stopped whooping his ass.

"Where you think you going?" I asked, grabbing her by the hair as she tried to turn the door knob. Pushing her head forward, she hit her head on the door, and I threw her to the ground. Not bothering to waste another second, I screwed on the silencer then shot and killed them both.

Grabbing my son's car seat, I stared down at him and he smiled at me. I casually walked outside like I didn't just commit a double homicide. B-Moore saw me walking and stepped out his truck.

"Burn it," I said before I strapped my son in the car. The first spot we were heading the hospital to make sure he was good.

"I miss you, little man," I told him, kissing his cheek and he started laughing. Damn it felt good to have Jr. back.

Chapter 19 Rich Boy

"**W**hy aren't you packed up? I told you to be ready when I got back from getting us a ride." I asked Rissa.

"I'm not going back to Columbus," Rissa said, and I stared at this bitch, not having time for her ass. She picked the wrong fucking time to hop on this stupid shit. When she told me let's go down to the A for a few weeks until things die down, I agreed because shit was hot as fuck in the city. I was running out of money though, and it's time to go back. Plus, that hoe ass detective been leaving threatening voicemails on my shit.

"Rissa, I don't have the energy to do this right now. We have to go back and I need to make shit right with Detective Johnson. The nigga probably think I ghosted him and is going to put a warrant out for my arrest?"

"So, you still thinking about snitching?" She shook her head as she walked around the Airbnb where we were staying.

"Do I have any other fucking choice? It's me or them niggas, and I'm not sitting it down for some jersey numbers, not for you or no fucking body!"

"When I met you, I thought you were a real nigga. Now, the more I'm around you, I'm starting to realize you're no street nigga, you're a fraud! A real street nigga knows there's risk and getting caught is one of them! You know I lost my brother for almost a decade because his best friend snitched on him. How could you think snitching is the best option? Let's just stay in the A and start over down here."

"How the fuck you expect me to start over? I'm a damn drug dealer, that shit don't come easy! I can't just fucking start over!"

"Well if I go back with you, I'm letting everyone know you're a snitch! It's either move here or be known in the hood as a rat! The choice is yours."

"What you just say to me, bitch?" I walked up on her. She folded her arms as if she wasn't terrified of a nigga and that made me feel some kind of way. If my own bitch didn't have fear in her when it came to me, how the fuck would these niggas in the streets do? I must have been going soft.

"You heard me, I'm not scared of you! Get your rat ass out this fucking hotel and go back to Columbus, you rat bitch!" Before I knew it, I was punching Rissa in her face. I didn't stop, not even when she was on the ground. I kept punching her and punching her as images of everyone who tried to play me came to my head.

"You think you can play me pussy?" I yelled as I continued punching and punching her. It wasn't until I got tired that I stopped.

"Rissa," I said as I stared down at her bloody face. She wasn't moving. I tried to shake her, but she wasn't getting up. "Baby, baby, get up please," I begged.

Placing two fingers on her neck, I searched for a pulse and didn't feel one.

"I fucked up, I killed her." I placed my hands on my head as I stared at her lethargic body. I cried as I realized what I did. I was alone in this world now, all because I let my anger get the best of me.

***

"Look it here, you been a hard one to get in touch with," Detective Robinson said. I should have known coming back home wasn't a smart idea. I've been back in Columbus for one week. I avoided coming back home for this very reason, but money was low and I had a stash spot built under the dog house in my backyard.

"You still stalking a nigga?"

"We had a deal. What's in the bag?" He asked, taking the book bag off my shoulder. I glared at the nigga angrily because I was tired of his ass. This personal vendetta he had was getting in the way of my money.

"Look it here, I hit the jackpot." He smiled at me.

"Now you robbing a nigga?"

"Let's just call it payment for you going MIA. I want something within 48 hours or your money won't be the only thing I'm taking. Your freedom will be gone too," Robinson said, backing up. He smiled at me, put his hand to his ear like he was holding a phone, then got in his car and drove off.

"Fuck!" I yelled. Shit changed just that quick. I was desperate, and all bets were off.

Still Caught Up With A Trap God

Chapter 20 Carmen

"**S**o, you're seriously going to ignore me?" Elijuan asked as we walked from out the classroom. It was the end of the day and today had been a long one. I seriously wanted to go home to my son and just relax.

"What do you want me to say? You fought my child's father, Elijuan, there's no way we can be friends. My loyalty will always be with him," I said, facing him as we walked outside of the school.

It was warm outside and the sun was shining, so I decided to bring out the Benz Raul bought for me when he really started seeing real money.

"Look, he stepped to me. What was I supposed to do? Our friendship means something to me, and if I'm being honest, I don't want the shit to end," he said, grabbing my hands. The sincerity was in his voice and his eyes.

In a different lifetime, I could see me and Elijuan being great friends and probably something more. Although Raulin and I weren't together anymore, I still felt as if he was it for me. He just needed to grow as a person more. I didn't want to be the wife of a man who was involved heavily in the streets. I couldn't see myself holding down a nigga if he were to go and do a bid. Nah, I saw more for my son and more for myself. I saw myself uplifting a king. I wasn't meant to be a girl to a street nigga, I was meant to be the wife of a man. So, until Raulin came like that, we weren't going to be together. Still, that didn't change the fact that my loyalty will always go to him.

"Look I, can't do this," I began to say.

The sound of a gunshot going off caused whatever set of words about to come from Elijuan's mouth to stop. People started to run and scream. Before I knew it, another shot went off and Elijuan fell on his face.

"Elijuan, oh my God!" I yelled. He had on a white shirt, so the blood soaked through. I could put two and two together to know he was shot. Taking out my cellphone, my hands shook uncontrollably as I called the police.

Putting the phone on speaker, I talked to the police as I applied pressure to the bullet hole in Elijuan's back. Someone must have called the school police because they were rushing over to where we were with first aid kits in their hands.

"What happened?" A caucasian, fat, male officer asked, bending down to me. His partner took out gauzes and applied them to the gunshot wound.

"Just keep your eyes open!" I cried. His eyes began to water and he tried to talk. "Don't talk, just hold on. You hear the ambulance, their close, hold on." I squeezed his hand. "Please don't let him die!" I cried to the police who were helping him.

"Calm down, ma'am, help is on the way," one of the officers said, trying to get me to calm down.

It wasn't working. I felt light headed and seeing all that blood made me sick.

***

I sat in a chair in the hospital waiting room, staring at my blood-stained hands. I rubbed my hands, desperately wishing I could get the blood off. I shook as I tried to get myself to calm down. I'd been there for hours and still hadn't received any updates on Elijuan.

"Carmen, OMG! Are you okay?" Jaliyah rushed into the hospital with Renz following behind her. I texted Jaliyah not too long ago, telling her I was at the hospital. I didn't want to be alone. She asked if I okay and I didn't respond because I was stuck in a twilight zone. Obviously, she was so worried, she called Renz.

"I'm fine. Someone was shooting on campus and Elijuan got shot. It could have been me!" My big brother wrapped his arms around me, and I cried into his chest.

"What happened?" I heard Raulin's voice and stepped out Renz's arms to bring my attention to him.

"You did it, didn't you?! You shot Elijuan, didn't you?! How could you when
I was standing so close to him! The bullet could have hit me, and I could have died!" I walked up on him and punched him in his chest as I cried. He grabbed my arms and stared at me. His jaw flexed, and I could tell he was angry. The security officer came over and told us we needed to calm down or we would have to leave, so I settled down some.

"You think I shot your nigga?" Raulin asked, letting go of my wrists. He stared at Renz then Jaliyah and finally back at me again.

"He's just my friend, but yes, I know you shot him. How else did you know to come here?" I questioned.

"I called both Raul and Renz when you told me you were at the hospital. You can't possibly think Raulin would do something like that, especially with you being so close," Jliyah said and that made me feel like shit.

"Look, I'm sorry-" I started to say to Raul, but he cut me off before I could finish.

"Looks like you traded one street nigga for another. I would never bring harm to you like that and you should know that. Where's my son?" Raul asked, looking at me like he was disgusted by me.

"He's with your mom," I told him and Raulin rushed out of the hospital doors.

"Raulin!" I called out to him, following him out the sliding doors. "Raulin!" I called again when he didn't stop.

"Fuck you want, Carmen?" He stopped to turn around and look at me.

"I'm sorry."

"Save that shit. You up here with this nigga while my mom got my baby, and after the nigga disrespected me in public. You chose your side, shorty, so stay over there."

He walked away, leaving me more sad than I already was.

Chapter 21 Raulin

P
ulling out the parking lot of the hospital, so many thoughts invaded my mental. One being how I could have lost my baby moms. When I got the frantic call from Jliyah saying Carmen was in the hospital, my heart dropped. I ain't know what the fuck was going on and neither did Jliyah. Imagine my surprise when I get there and she coming at me about shooting this nigga. She had the game fucked up, and I honestly meant what I said, I was cool on her ass.

Pulling up to my mom's crib, I used my key to unlock her door. When I walked in, mom dukes was stretched out on the sofa sleep and Quincy was in his bassinet in front of her. He must've felt my presence because he woke up crying.

"I got him, ma. Where's his diaper bag?" I asked as she woke up.

"Right here. What brings you here? Carmen texted and asked if I could keep him tonight."

"You good, I got him. She's at the hospital," I told my mom, picking my son up out of the bassinet and paced the floor with him. I smiled at him. Damn, I couldn't believe I was really a father.

"Put my grandson down real quick and let me talk to you," Ma said, sitting up on the couch. I did what she asked and had a seat next to her.

"Talk to me, son. You alright?"

"Yea, dukes, I'm fine. Why you ask me that?"

"Well, because you came from me. I carried you inside of my body then had you, plus raised you. I know when something's not sitting right with you."

"It ain't shit, ma-" I began to say, but she smacked me on the back of my head before I could get another word out.

"Boy, I told you about that disrespectful ass mouth of yours."

"So, you can cuss but I can't?"

"Exactly! Now go head and finish telling me what's going on." I shook my head and let out a chuckle. My moms was off the hook. This is how she was all the time.

"Look, mom, me and Carmen having problems."

"Why?"

"She claim it's because of my lifestyle."

"Well I don't blame her. That's not something a woman wants to deal with for the rest of her life."

"What you talking about, momma?" I asked. I never told my moms exactly what I did.

"What, you think I'm stupid? You thought I didn't know what the fuck was going on? I know what you're involved in, son, just like I knew what your brother was involved in. Do better, son, before you lose a great woman behind a lifestyle that took your brother. With that being said, I'm going to sleep. Make sure you stop to get him more milk."

She got up from the couch, kissed Quincy, then headed towards her bedroom.

***

Carrying the car seat inside of the grocery store, I chuckled as I thought back to how dukes just lowkey let my ass have it back at the house.

"Damn, I don't even know what kind of milk to get," I said out loud as I stood in the aisle at the grocery store in front of all the options. This shit was new to a nigga. Only recently did Carmen want to start Quincy on milk. She was breastfeeding at first.

"Here, let me help you. This is the best kind," I heard. Next to me was a cold yellow bone. "This the best one." She handed me the can of milk and I took this as the time to take her in. Shawty had a bun on top of her head. She was rocking a black, basic sweat suit and wore the latest pair of ones that had just dropped. I couldn't lie, she still looked good.

"Thanks, shorty. What's your name?"

"Rose," she said as she walked away.

"Hold on, shorty, you ain't gon' give me your numbe,r so I can properly thank you for helping a nigga out?"

"Where's your phone?" I gave her my phone and watched her put her number in it. Her phone started ringing seconds later. "Just in case you thought you were about to stand me up and skip out on giving me that free meal."

Still Caught Up With A Trap God

She smiled, handed me my phone and walked away. I chuckled and walked in the other direction where the checkout lines were.

Chapter 22 Renz

"**W**ord? So, you found out where that hoe ass detective stay?" I asked Mike Mike as we spoke on the phone.

"Yea, it took me a while. They be having 12 shit extra hidden."

"Say less. It's already been enough said over the phone, I'll meet up with you later," I told him and hung up.

"What was that about?" MiMi asked, coming up behind me and wrapping her arms around my waist. I love MiMi's ass and there was nothing I wouldn't do for her, including killing a detective who was on some Fatal Attraction shit. At the same time, the less she knew, the better.

"That was business, nothing you need to worry your beautiful ass about."

"I heard what you said. I hope you're not going to go after Detective Robinson. I already put a complaint in with his supervisor," she said, causing me to turn around and face her.

"When you do that shit? Since when you start dealing with the pigs?"

"I saw him again when I was taking Amara to her doctor's appointment."

"What? Why the fuck you didn't say shit? This nigga is getting too out of control," I said, shaking my head. This nigga must really see me as a hoe ass nigga, I was ending this shit.

"I didn't want you to overreact, just please let this go. I already put a complaint in with his supervisor."

"What do you think that's going to do, MiMi? You have proof of the nigga stalking you?" I asked her, and she look around, avoiding eye contact with me.

"It's your word against his. That shit won't matter unless you have proof. I'm handling him," I told her.

"Handle him how? I thought you were done with that lifestyle."

"Protecting my family is not a lifestyle. I'm handling him and that's final." Before she could get a word in, a big ass commotion stopped her words.

"Police!" I heard.

"Get Amara and call my lawyer." Niomi rushed out the room. I headed out the room and met the police at the top of the stairs.

"Put your hands in the air, asshole!" FBI agents and police officers charged at me with their guns pointed. Doing what they said, I put my hands in the air. A black male FBI agent threw me to the ground, being extra and shit.

"Lorenzo White, you have the right to remain silent. Anything you say will be used against you in a court of law…."

"I know my fucking rights!" I barked as they brought me to my feet.

"Where are you taking him?" MiMi asked and I glanced at her. She had tears running down her face as she rocked Amara back and forth.

"Call my lawyer, MiMi. Stop crying, I'll be straight," I told her and the cops took me out of my home.

"Lorenzo White, it feels good seeing you in here. You need anything? Well, actually, I don't give a fuck what you need," Detective Robinson said and I glared at him. I wish I wasn't in this damn interrogation room, I would strangle the bitch nigga with my bare fucking hands.

"Pussy ass nigga, what the fuck am I here for?"

"Armed robbery-" He was interrupted by my lawyer walking in.

"I'm here to take my client home."

"Home? We have a witness that he was involved in the robbery at National bank a few months ago."

"You will get your day in court. In the meantime, my client has made bail and we're leaving."

"Don't get comfortable, Mr. White, I'll be seeing you soon."

"Indeed, you will," I told him, giving him a warning without actually saying much.

"You think they really got proof?" I asked my lawyer. We rode in his car as he was taking me home.

"Listen, if they have a witness, things could get bad. My best advice will be to find the witness," he informed, and I didn't say anything else about it.

I was too deep in thought trying to figure out who the witness could be and how they knew about the bank job.

Chapter 23 Diggy

"*So, everything's fine with my son, doc?*" *I asked after the doctor evaluated Jr.*

"Yes, he's fine and up to date on all his shots. We will see you in a few months for his next appointment, just stop at the desk in the front to schedule it."

After the hospital visit, we headed straight home. Raven was nowhere in sight and that was a good thing. Putting Jr. in his and Rayna's room, I headed to our bedroom to see if Raven was in there. She was stretched out on the bed with Rayna in front of her.

"Ray, wake up." I kissed her on the cheek and her eyes opened.

"Today must be a good day, I get a kiss and all." She gave me a small smile, looked down at Rayna who was still sleeping and kissed her forehead.

"I have to show you something. Grab Rayna and come on," I told her. She rubbed her eyes, grabbed Rayna, then stood up and followed behind me.

*"Wait! How! Oh my God! My baby!" She
screamed, putting Rayna in my arms then heading over to
Jr's bed. She picked him up and kissed all over his face.
"Baby, oh my baby." Tears rolled down her face and Jr.
laughed.*

*I took in the scene in front of me and smiled; my
family was complete again.*

"Demontae? You don't hear me talking to you?"
Rayven asked, snapping me out of reminiscing on the day I
brought my son back home.

"What, Ray, damn?"

"What? What you mean what? You told me you
were out of the life! How the hell you out of the life when I
just picked you up from jail!" She was irate as fuck and I
understood why. I was mad too.

"I got picked up and arrested for the bank job we
did that you helped with! They said they have a witness and
I'm trying to figure out who the fuck the witness is."

"You think it's a scare tactic?"

"Nah, they wouldn't have wasted time to make an arrest if they didn't have no hardcore evidence. Someone's talking, I just don't know who."

"Who all knows about it ?"

"You, Renz, Niomi, Raul, RichBoy and me."

"Damonte, be real with me. Is there anything you are involved in that I don't know about?"

"Come on, Ray. What will make you ask me some shit like that?"

"I just wanna know if anything's gonna come back to bite us in the ass later. You're out the game, right?" She asked as we pulled into the driveway of our home. She parked the car, then turned it off before staring at me intensely.

"Alright look, sometimes I hold some of Raul's money for him."

"What the fuck you mean *hold?* You holding his money just because?"

"Look, I'm just cleaning his money for him through my shop," I told her, coming clean. Holding secrets is what almost got her killed and my son taken.

"Wow! I can't believe you! For how long?"

"A few months now."

"Wow! So you come at me and make me feel like shit about keeping secrets and you been keeping secret for months about you still being in the fucking game, nigga!" She got out the car, slammed the door and walked in the house.

"Fuck!" I banged my hand against the dashboard. Shit was spiraling out of control. I thought once I got my son back, it would be better, but shit is just falling apart. I didn't know what a nigga's next move was, but I had to move fast.

Getting out of the car, I hopped in my Benz and headed to Renz's house. We had some shit to discuss we needed to get to the bottom of who the fuck the rat was.

The ride to Renz's house was quicker than ever have before and that was because a nigga was on ten. I had to talk to my right-hand man to see if he had any clue what the fuck was going on because I was oblivious as fuck.

"What's good, nigga? I'm assuming 12 came and swooped your ass up too," Renz said, opening the door. He stepped out the way and I walked in.

"Hell yeah! What the fuck is going on? A nigga been able to stay out of 12's rearview mirror all this time, how the fuck we get caught up over a bank robbery we did a minute ago? Our hands been clean. We got to figure some shit out. You talk to Raul?" I asked, pacing the floor back and forth.

"Yeah, I called his ass right after you called saying you were on your way. The nigga should be pulling up any minute. We gotta figure this shit out."

The words had just left his mouth when there was a knock on the door. Renz went to open up the door and we saw Raul on the other side."

"I'm pretty sure you know the Feds came and scooped us up, so I know they got your ass too. We gotta figure out who the fuck ratted us out," Renz said and the room got quiet.

"RichBoy, that's the nigga who ratted us out. I knew the nigga was lingering around for some reason. I'ma murder that hoe ass nigga!" Raul said.

"Fuck you talking 'bout, Raul?" I asked.

"Weeks ago, the nigga popped up at the trap talking about he felt like he was owed more money because of the bank job we did. Him popping up unexpectedly wasn't adding up, so I closed down the spot. Never in a million years did I think the nigga would turn into a fucking rat. I'm the one who brought him into this shit, so I'm gonna have to handle it. I'll holla at you niggas later," he said and the nigga was out. Dapping Renz up, I left too. I had personal issues at home with my woman I had to deal with.

Chapter 24 Rich Boy

At first a nigga was feeling fucked up because of the pressure Detective Robinson put on me. Plus, I was having nightmares, seeing Rissa and shit. I couldn't believe my anger got the best of me, and I killed the woman I love. When all this was over, Detective Robinson was going to pay for what he did.

I was still trying to figure out how I could bring that nigga Raul out of hiding since he close down his trap. That's when I came up with the idea to shoot Carmen. I already knew where her school was. I waited outside her school for hours, not knowing her class schedule. When I finally saw her, I knew it was now or never. Imagine how irate I was when I missed her ass and shot some other nigga. Now I was back to square fucking one.

I said fuck it and just told detective Robinson I will testify against them about the bank robbery we did. He said that it wouldn't work, but we can scare them into confessing. I knew them niggas wouldn't do no shit like that, but I just followed his lead. Just like I knew, the shit didn't work. Now Detective Robinson was breathing down my neck about finding another way. The nigga was getting worse the longer them niggas were out and that shit only made me more paranoid because my freedom was on the line.

I was back to square one. That was until Diamond called me and asked that I pull up on her. I was still in tune with what happens in the neighborhood, so I knew Raulin and her ass were on the outs. Thinking she probably wanted revenge for how he had Tanisha and her girls beat her ass, I agreed to meet the bitch. Pulling up to her house, I texted to tell her I was outside and waited for her to come out.

"Damn, he had them bitches fuck you up," I said, shaking my head when she slid into the passenger side of my ride. Her face was bruised like a motherfucker.

"Look, it's no secret you and Raul not cool anymore. I say we come together and bring that hoe ass nigga down."

"Who said I have any problems with Raul? Who said I want to bring the nigga down?" I asked. Part of me still ain't trust the bitch.

"Cut the bullshit, RichBoy! Everyone in the hood knows Raul stopped fucking with you and you haven't been making as much money as you had when you were fucking with him. I say with him out the way, you will be the top nigga in the hood."

"What you got planned?"

"I know where his stash spot at. I say we hit him up and take everything he got. If he don't have any product, then he don't have a way to make some money."

"And what you get out of helping me out?"

"Other than watching that grimy motherfucker lose everything he has, I want 50% of everything that we get from the spot."

"Word, where is it? Give me the address, and I'll handle it. I'll bring you your half."

"Nigga, get serious. I ain't no green bitch. I'm going with you."

"Alright look, I'll be back around three in the morning, and we'll go."

"Three in the morning?"

"Yea, that's when shit will be unexpected. More than likely, nobody will be guarding shit."

"Alright, I'll see you then." She got out of my ride and I watched her ass jiggle. Diamond was a bad bitch, and she knew it.

***

It was three in the morning exactly when I pulled up to Diamond's crib. Honking once, I waited patiently for Diamond to exit her home.

"Damn, it's cold as shit out here," she said, sliding into my car.

"It's hot as hell, you trippin. Where we going?"

"Zanesville."

"Damn, this nigga stash spot in Zansville?" I asked. That was a good 45 minutes away from the city.

"Yea. Well, it's actually quite smart," she said, and I just nodded my head. The rest of the ride was quiet. I couldn't tell you what Diamond was thinking about, but I was thinking about how I was about to come up. Raul thought he was that nigga because he got put on by them niggas Renz and Diggy, but I was about to show that nigga who was scout to be the head nigga in charge. The nigga lucky we're only robbing his ass. Soon enough though, Detective Robinson was going to get rid of him. As I thought about Detective Robson, a thought came to my head. I will take most of the product for myself, keeps some there, murder Diamond and send Detective Robinson the location to Raul's stash-spot, so he could have a murder and drug charge.

"This it?" I asked. The spot was nothing more than a little storage spot.

"Yes. Wouldn't think this spot holds drugs, would you?" Diamond asked.

I stepped out the car. Once she did the same, I took out my strap and pointed it in her direction. Raul was a dumb ass nigga for trusting a bitch with the location of his stash spot. I don't give a fuck what history they shared. The fact that the nigga lacked intellect was about to be my personal come up.

"I should have known I couldn't trust you," she said.

"The same way I can't trust you. You want me to believe a nigga as paranoid as Raul let you know where he stashed his money and work? You trying set me up! Where the fuck are them niggas, I'm not pussy!" I barked, looking around.

"How am I going to set you up? Did you fucking forget that grimy shit Raul did to me? I want that nigga suffering just like you! I want that nigga broke just like you! You're fucking trippin', we ain't got time for this shit. Let's get what we came for and get the fuck out of here!" She said.

I looked at her and put my gun down. She was right, I came here for one reason. Regardless, she wouldn't be walking away tonight with her life. At the end of the day, I wasn't sharing shit with her ass. She didn't deserve it. A nigga definitely wasn't about to have her ass turn snake on me and put it out there that I was the one who hit his stash spot. Raul was not the kind of nigga to be fucked with. Even though I was a gutter nigga, I knew if I kept this bitch breathing, he would come looking for me, and I couldn't have it. I was going need an army to go to war with them niggas. I had a few niggas but none that stood a chance against them.

Still Caught Up With A Trap God

Walking to the storage container, I screwed my silencer on my gun and shot the locks off. Entering the building, I used the light on my phone to locate the light in the storage container and turned it on. I was in fucking heaven when I came face to face with what was in front of me. There were boxes on top of boxes lined up against the wall. Going over to the first one, I opened it and the first thing I saw was that white girl stacked up nicely.

"Jack fucking pot!" I said, followed by Diamond giggling.

"So, how are we gonna get all this shit in the car?" Diamond asked and I looked at her.

"How the fuck else? Let's go before this nigga come looking. I don't know if he gotta lookout or what, but I ain't risking it, so get the fucking boxes and carry this shit to the car so we can be out."

I grabbed the first box and headed back to my truck. I could hear footsteps coming behind me and knew it was Diamond. Not saying a word, I went back into the storage, grabbed another box and put it in my trunk. We kept doing that until it was about 3 boxes left.

"Keep the rest here." I looked at Diamond and she appeared skeptical.

"What for?"

"'Cause no more could fit in my car, now bring your ass on," I told her. When she started following me, I turned around and pointed my gun at her.

"You know I could never let you live after this, right?" I asked her. She looked at me and shook her head with tears rolling down her face.

"I knew I should've never trusted you. I knew you were a snake!"

"That I may be, but you are now dead!"

Boom!

I shot her and got in my ride. The next thing I did was call Detective Robinson. He didn't answer right away, so I left a voicemail.

"I have intel on the nigga Raul's stash spot. I'm about to text you the location. Get there ASAP. From what I hear, it's a lot of product in there," I said and hung up.

A smile graced my face as I thought about how a nigga was about to come up.

Chapter 25 Niomi

Over hearing Renz talking about basically getting rid of Detective Robinson had me on edge. I know how much my husband loved me and I knew what he would do to secure my happiness and safety. I didn't want my husband to take the risk of killing a detective and going to jail. No, I couldn't have that. I needed him. Amara needed him. After thinking long and hard, I came up with an idea. It's been a minute since the detective has popped up on me, but I knew he was after my husband and that, I couldn't have.

"You sure this will work?" I asked the private investigator as I sat across from him at his small practice. He had just given me a recording device and agreed to follow me.

"Yes. When you're about to leave the house, you call me and I'll come follow you. When he pops up, we will have the pictures for proof."

"What's the recording device for?"

"It won't be admissible in court. It's not legal to record, it's just to bring along with the pictures I take to get the ball rolling," Jake, the private investigator said.

I started to say something until I glanced at the TV. It was a video of police outside of Raulin and Carmen's home. Raul had handcuffs on and the caption on the TV read: *Suspect arrested for murder.*

"What? I have to go?"

"Should I follow you now?" Jake asked, regaining my attention.

"No, I'll call you." I thanked him again and rushed home.

Heading in the house, Carmen was on the couch while Renz comforted her.

"I take it y'all watched the news?" I asked, sitting on the couch next to Carmen. Giving her a hug, I looked at Renz.

"The kids are upstairs sleep. Stay with her. I have to get a lawyer down to my nigga and see what the fuck is going on."

I nodded and he left out the door. I looked at Carmen and wrapped my arms around her.

"He promised he wouldn't leave me to raise his son on his own. We never even got the chance to be together again. All because I was being stubborn. If I would have been home, none of this would have happened."

She cried from the depth of her soul as I just rocked her back and forth. I hated that this was happening to them. It was like our family couldn't get a break.

***

"What time is it?" I asked, rolling over after feeling the other side of the bed sink down. Renz look tired. He left hours ago and was just now coming back.

"A little after 12. I didn't mean to wake you."

"It's cool. What did they say about Raul?"

"The nigga out. He been fucking with some bitch and come to find out, she a pig. He was with her the day of the murder all day, and she vouched for him. Who would ever think a fucking pig would save his ass from murder?"

"Wait, Raulin's dating someone?" I heard. Renz and I turned our attention towards the doorway where Carmen was standing, looking hurt.

"Damn, I thought you were sleep, baby sis. I wouldn't have mentioned it. This a conversation for you and Raul to have," Renz said.

Carmen looked at him, then me and turned around to head in the direction of her room.

"Damn. The last thing I wanted to do was make their shit more complicated," Raul said, shaking his head.

I nodded my head, gave him a kiss on the cheek and blew out a breath of frustration. I was rooting for Carmen and Raul. They had a story not too many people would understand, but I was a hopeless romantic. I was in love with the idea of love and hoped they could work it out.

***

Three days, that's how long it's been since meeting with Jake. I made sure to call him and have him follow me every time I left the house. I also made sure to keep the recording device he gave me tucked in my purse. I had already called Jake and let him know I had errands today. He just texted me and let me know he was outside the gates of my home. Grabbing Amara, I strapped her in her car seat and headed out. The first stop I had to make was to

Amara's doctor's appointment. Renz was originally supposed to come, but he had important business to attend to with the moving company. Of course, he didn't want to miss her doctor's appointment and I told him it was fine.

Pulling up to the hospital, I checked my surroundings. I had an eerie feeling and didn't know why. Hearing a beep, I looked in the direction I heard the sound from and noticed Jake. That made me feel better. Opening the backseat to the car, I took Amara out and when I turned around, just like before, there was Detective Robinson.

"You look beautiful," he said and touched my face.

I stepped back and glared at him as I held Amara tighter. I secretly put my hand in my purse and turned on my recorder. Raul had bought me a gun and right now, I wish I would have brought it with me. He was getting out of hand.

"You know, Niomi, I'm done playing around. For some reason, your husband is a lucky motherfucker, so instead of getting rid of him, I'll take you." He grabbed my arm and I snatched away. He pulled out a gun, pointed it at Amara and I cried. The gun wasn't noticeable. I glanced around, trying to make contact with someone, but the few people in the parking lot wasn't paying any attention to us.

"You're a detective. You really think you can get away with kidnapping me and my daughter?"

"Yes, let's go." He forcefully grabbed my arm. Amara started to fuss and I looked down at my baby girl, hoping Jake would somehow come and save us. I didn't want this sick man to take us. If he did, I knew we wouldn't see my husband, Raven, Diggy, Carmen, Raul and especially my sister, ever again.

"Please don't!" I cried.

"What are you doing? Let her g.?" Jake had a gun pointed at him and he let go before glancing back at me then bringing his attention fully to Jake again.

"Everything is fine my man, I'm a detective," he said and Jake looked at me.

"Get in the car, Niomi," he said, never taking his gun off Detective Robinson.

"You better not move, Niomi!"

He barked, pointing his gun at Jake. By this time, people were starting to run and I even saw some on the phone. Taking the chance, I slowly backed up, headed to my car and got in the front seat still carrying Amara. I didn't have the time to put her in the car seat.

Boom! Boom! The sound of gunshots followed by screams, making me stop. Amara was crying and I was scared. Looking behind me, I saw both Jake and Detective Robinson lying on the ground.

" Jakeeeeeeee!" I cried out.

Chapter 26 Raul

"*I fuck with you.*" *I glanced over, kissing the top of Rose's head. Nah, she wasn't my girl, but shawty had a vibe to her. I been kicking it with her since I met her at the grocery store a few weeks back.*

"I fuck with you too," she said, leaning up and giving me a kiss. We fucked earlier today and the way she was kissing me had a nigga ready for another round.

My phone ringing stopped me from telling her to take off her clothes.

"What's good, nigga?"

"I got pulled last night."

"And you out already?" I asked one of my little niggas, hopping up.

Something about a nigga going to jail and getting right back out didn't sit well with me. Turning towards Rose, I headed towards the front door and went out of it. Shorty was cool, but I wasn't about to have the conversation I needed to have with my little nigga in front of her.

"Come on, nigga, you know I'm a clean nigga. Only thing they could get me on was driving with no Ls. I paid bail."

"They ask about me?" I asked. A nigga was paranoid since I put two and two together about RichBoy. The nigga turned rat. We were able to still be free 'cause we paid top dollar for the best lawyers there are. Still, that nigga knew too much about me and I wasn't taking no chances. The nigga been MIA, but I knew he would show up again, and I was going to murk they ass.

"Hell nah, why would they?"

"Some other shit? What's good though?"

"When I got pulled, it was because I was trying to follow the bitch Diamond and RichBoy?"

"Fuck you say?" I asked as I racked my brain on why they would be together. Even before they never fucked with each other, the only common denominator was me. They were plotting.

*"Fuck! The storage spot!" I barked into the phone.
One day, I had Diamond's ass help me put my product up
since it was late night, and I was with her. Shorty was
really a nigga's best friend at one point in time, so I never
did change shit up.*

"What about it?"

*"Meet me there!" I said into the phone then hung
up. Jogging to my car, I was about to hop in my ride when
the sound of cop sirens and their cars swooping into Rose's
driveway stopped me.*

*"Freeze! Put your hands in the air," I heard. Not
taking no, chances I did what they asked. Rose came from
outside her home, took my gun, and I stared at this bitch,
knowing she was the reason for all these cops to be here
right now.*

*"You have the right to remain silent. Anything you
say may be use against you..." she began to say, but I cut
the bitch off.*

*"I know my rights, pig." I look at her disgusted.
This bitch was the one thing I hated other than a snake, and
that was a pig. I saw the hurt on her face, but a nigga ain't*

give a fuck. Looking around, I was surrounded by news reporters, SWAT and more police. They were surrounding my ass like I was El Chapo.

***

"You might as well confess to the murder of Diamond Williams and to the three boxes full of drugs we found. I'll give you a deal if you tell me everything I want to hear about Lorenzo White."

Laughing, I shook my head for more than one reason. One being this nigga thought he could make me snitch. Second being this nigga said three boxes of work when I know for sure I had boxes on top of boxes. Diamond being dead and the fact my little homie told me he saw her with RichBoy let me know all I needed to know. The most comical shit is Detective Robinson said he trying to arrest me for Diamond's murder, and I knew he was reaching.

"Something amusing?" He asked.

"I didn't murder Diamond, and I know nothing about some drugs."

"Let's cut the bullshit, Raulin!" He banged his hand on the wooden table as I chuckled before leaning back in the chair.

"It's no bullshit. I been with Rose for the last 48 hours," I said with a chuckle.

The color drained from his face and soon after, the door to the investigation room opened. In walked Rose, followed by my lawyer.

"He's free to go," Rose said as her and the hoe ass detective shared a look. I looked at the badge around her neck and gave her a smirk.

"Thanks for the pussy, detective." I walked pass her and followed my lawyer out of the police station. I saw Renz as soon as we exited.

"How's you know to call my lawyer?"

"The shit was all over the news, but shit, Carmen called," he told me and I nodded my head. The lawyer came over, shook our hands and left.

"Who they trying to say you murdered?"

"The bitch Diamond. Only reason I'm out now is 'cause I was with the bitch Rose when the shit went down. The whole time, the bitch a pig," I told him, shaking my head. We got into his ride and he laughed.

"Damn! Who the fuck killed Diamond?" He asked.

"RichBoy. And he stole my work. I'ma murk that nigga, he tried to set me up," I told him.

We ain't speak on the shit anymore, we both knew what I had to do. RichBoy just caused me to take a major loss. As bad as I wanted to find the nigga, I would have to lay low knowing 12 had their sights on me.

"Someone keeps blowing you up," Carmen said, taking a seat next to me, snapping me out of the flashback of me going to jail a few days ago. I came over to Reno's crib to be around my family with all the havoc that's been going on. I just wanted to kick it with my babymomma and my son.

Hitting the ignore button on Rose again, I looked at Carmen. She was so beautiful. I'm not going to lie, I wanted my family back, but I wasn't sure I was exactly what they needed right now. I had to come correct if I wanted to get them back.

"Why you didn't come back to the crib? I told you it ain't shit for me to find a little spot."

"I don't want to be in that big home alone."

"Shit, you can always move back and live on one side while I live on the other," I told her. My son giggling got our attention. We both smiled as I held him in my arms and rocked him back and forth. *Damn, he deserves better,* I thought to myself.

"So, was it serious?" Carmen asked, regaining my attention.

"Was what serious?"

"Your relationship with the cop bitch!" Carmen screamed and our son started crying.

"Man, calm your ass down! Fuck is you screaming for?"

"Because you got me fucked up! How the fuck are you laying up with a bitch? You just don't give a fuck about your family, do you?!" She yelled and I let out an angry chuckle. Carmen had me fucked up.

"Man, shut your stupid ass up. I didn't walk away from my family! You walked your funky ass away from me and made sure to take my son with your stupid ass! She was just my homie like the nigga you shared classes with was yours," I told her ass and brought my attention back to my son. He had stopped crying and by this time, he was just staring at me.

"Did you fuck her?" She asked, and I ignored her ass. She knew she really didn't want to know the answer to that question.

"Now you can't hear, nigga?!" Her crazy ass began to pace the floor.

"Yes, I fucked the bitch."

"Wow! Your trifling ass never learns. I hope you used protection."

"I did." I shrugged. Her ass was in her feelings now, but that was on her. What the fuck did she expect? I was a man with needs. She shouldn't have asked the question. She wanted a nigga to be real and I was.

"Yea, okay. Keep acting nonchalant about it and watch me go out here and have a revenge fuck." She barked and my teeth clenched at the thought of her fucking someone else.

"You claim you want a nigga to change his ways, but that hoeing behavior gon' have a nigga in a box and your hoe ass in the hospital. I'll kill over that pussy," I told her.

I kissed my son, put him in her hands and was out. A nigga had too much drama going on. The last thing I wanted to deal with is my baby mama drama.

Chapter 27 Raven

I know I kept my secrets, but the fact Diggy kept a secret about cleaning Raulin's drug money didn't sit right with me. Here I was, comfortable, thinking he was a legit business man and we were free from all illegal activities. Knowing my husband was still a part of the game had me on edge. Especially since the police were already knocking on our door, trying to lock up Diggy, Renz and Raul.

"What's good, beautiful, how you sleep?" Diggy asked.

Coming into the bedroom, he had a tray full of food and my favorite drink, apple juice. I smiled because my husband was definitely one of the sweetest men I have encountered. The grey sweat pants he had on showed his dick and my mouth watered as I thought about the last time we had sex. It's been weeks. His abs glistened and his curly hair was ruff. he must have been in our home gym working out.

"I'd rather have you for breakfast," I told him, being honest.

"Come hop in the shower with me."

Putting the tray of food on the dresser, he pulled me off the bed and led us to the bathroom. I stripped out of my clothes as he turned the shower water on. Once he got the shower on the right temperature, he stripped out his sweats and his dick sprang to life. My mouth watered as I look at it. My husband was blessed it was big, thick and pretty dick. I got in the shower and he got in behind me. He placed kisses down the back of my neck and did the same to my shoulder blade. I moaned as chills rose on my body.

"Damn…" I moaned out as he belligerently grabbed my hair and bit down on my shoulder blade. He then used the other hand to play in my pussy.

Before I could process my next thought, Diggy slid inside of me like he was on a baseball team.

"Fuck…" We moaned out in unison.

Knowing how my husband likes for me to fuck him back, I started throwing my ass back and he caught it. He smacked my ass a few times and then wrapped his hands around my hair. He sucked on my earlobe and before I knew it, I was coming.

"You know I'm still mad at you for keeping secrets," I told Diggy as I rubbed my hand threw his curly hair. He was the love of my life and I couldn't imagine life without him in it.

"Yea, that's understandable. It was never my intention to go behind your back with the shit, I'm just a... well *was* a street nigga. Raul came to me stressing about needing a way to clean money, and I thought it would be easy money and beneficial to my nigga. I get that I'm a family man now and you and the kids are above everything. I want us to have a successful marriage and that means there are no more secrets between the both of us. I'm officially done with that shit. I give you my word." He kissed my lips and I smiled.

No, we weren't perfect. We been through a lot together, but what was perfect? Nothing. Every obstacle Diggy and I overcame was another story we could tell our kids about what was really love.

"I love you, Demontae. I'm sorry I almost ruined our family forever," I cried as I thought about Jr. almost being gone forever. I was glad to have the husband that I have. He did what he was supposed to and brought my baby back.

"Don't think about that shit, he's fine. We're fine. We both just need to understand how detrimental keeping secrets can be," he said, and I nodded my head.

I thought back on our life. Since fifteen years old, it's been us. I watched this man grow right in front of my eyes, and I was in love with him even more. He was no longer a trap god. He was a grown ass man and he'd never been more sexier than he is now. After a pregnant pause, I stared in his eyes.

"Thank you for making this change for me. I know it wasn't easy, but I definitely appreciate you."

"I wish a nigga could physically give you the world, but since I can't, I'll do anything to make you happy. I love you, real shit, Ray."

Chapter 28 Carmen

"**H**ow are you holding up?" I asked Elijuan as I helped him get in the car. I'd just picked him up from the hospital. Due to complications, they kept him longer than expected.

"I been better if I'm speaking honestly. This not the first time a nigga been shot though," he stated when we finally got in the car.

"Really?" I side-eyed him as I pulled off from in front of the hospital.

"Hell yea. Just like before, I'm going to find out who it was that exactly shot me then me and my family are going to handle that shit."

"What does that mean?" I asked.

"What do you think?" I briefly looked his way again and for the first time, I saw that look in his eyes. It was the same look my brother and Raulin carried.

"Let me ask you something, and I need you to be honest."

"A nigga ain't never lie to you before, and I'm not going to start now."

"Are you a street nigga?"

"What's a street nigga?"

He let out a cocky laugh, but I wasn't in the mood to play. This was a serious ass topic and he needed to get to talking. Pulling over on the side of the street, I put the car in park, folded my arms and waited for him to speak. He rubbed his right hand across the top of his head then put his hand up in a surrender motion.

"Okay, look. Yea, I'm in the streets. My dad was one of the deadliest niggas back in Cali where we from. He's a smart man. He forced me and my brothers to get a degree, so if the law ever came knocking, we were on some official shit. Moms moved us down here when my father got locked up for some drug shit a few years ago To be with my aunt. I'm not even sure why I'm telling you this shit 'cause this type of information could fuck up a nigga's, life but I want more with you, Carmen. You do something to a nigga I can't explain," he told me and I sat there flabbergasted. All this time he was laying in the hospital, I felt guilt. Even though Raul said he had nothing to do with shooting Elijuan, I wasn't so sure, but now I was thinking he told the truth.

"This is too much. I can't be with you like that, Elijuan. Shit may be complicated with my child's father, but he's the one who owns my heart like it's a trademark. On top of that, I could have been shot because of some shit you got going on! That bullet was clearly meant for you because of the shit you're involved in. I could have died and left behind my son! I just can't," I said, shaking my head. I wasn't sure why these were the type of men I attracted, but at this point, I was feeling disgusted when it came to dealing with hood niggas. They came with baggage I wasn't willing to carry.

"So, what are you saying, Carmen?"

"It's best that after today, we don't speak," I told him.

He looked at me with hurt eyes, but I didn't care. There were no emotional ties to Elijuan, so walking away from him would be a lot simpler than it is walking away from Raulin.

***

"Are you okay, baby sis?" Niomi asked, taking a seat next to me on the sofa.

I was sitting in the dark crying, thinking about my life. This was not how I thought Raulin and I would be. My heart, my soul, and my body craved for him, but my son and I's safety was a lot more important.

"I just thought after all the bullshit I went through with Raulin, we would be happy now."

"Life ain't easy and love ain't either. It takes a lot of trials and tribulations to get to experience the happiness. Let me ask you something. Are you ready to walk away?"

"Of course not! I just can't risk me and my son because Raulin is still infatuated with the streets. He already done put us in harm's way. He just got arrested and it could have been forever. He would have left me and his son out here alone."

"You know you would never be alone. I get that, but I will say this. It took me loving your brother to fully understand this. Loving someone's not easy. When you love someone and truly love someone, you have to love what comes with them. Is it wrong for you to want Raul out of the streets? Hell no! I wanted the same thing with Renz. What I will say is before it was you, it was the streets, that's all he knew. That's how he was able to survive to this long. How he was able to provide for himself. They're what makes him Raulin. Leaving them may not be as easy as you think. I say you sit down and have a talk with him. A real conversation so you can understand things from his point of view."

She kissed my forehead then got up and began to walk away. She stopped then turned around and looked at me.

"Forgiveness is a strong word, but sometimes it is worth it. Look at me. I lost my memory and never got it back because of the man I love, yet he filled my head with so many new memories of happiness, I don't care. True love only happens once in a lifetime." She gave me a smile then headed back upstairs.

I sat there with everything she said on my mind. I hated to say it, but what she said made a lot of sense.

***

"What's good, you look beautiful," Raulin said, answering the door.

He kissed my cheek and move to the side. He grabbed the bags out of my hand as I walked into the house.

"Your bitch not here, is she?" I asked and he shook his head as I headed to the kitchen.

"I ain't got no bitch and if I did, I would never disrespect you by bringing her into our home."

I nodded my head as I took him in. Raul was fine as fuck and he knew it. The grey shirt he had on and sweat shorts were a basic ass outfit, but he made the shit look like he was about to walk down the runway wearing a million-dollar outfit.

"Hope you hungry because I'm making you breakfast," I told him as I started to take food out groceries bags he put on the kitchen counter.

"I don't know about that. I'm a little nervous. You trying to poison a nigga?" He let out a cocky laugh as he sat on the counter top.

"Raulin, get your funky ass off my damn kitchen counter!" I barked. He knew I didn't play that shit.

"My bad, I know how you are about this damn kitchen." He hopped off the counter and I turned towards the sink to wash my hands. Before I felt his hand on my waist, I smelled his cologne. That damn Tom Ford gets me every time. He kissed my neck and I smiled. I couldn't deny that I missed him.

"You know you a beautiful motherfucker, right?" He asked and I stepped to the side.

This wasn't what I was here for. Niomi and I's conversation weighed heavy on my mind. I hated to admit it, but I never really sat and tried to listen to Raul. He was the head of this family, which means he took everyone's weight and carried it on his back.

"Talk to me."

"About what ?" He went into the refrigerator, grabbed a water, then brought his attention back to me.

"Look, I'm no fan of the lifestyle you choose to live, but everyone needs someone to vent to. I rather you vent to me."

"Nah…" He said, shaking his head.

"Who else are you going to vent to? You know I'm not going to tell you what you want to hear, but I'm going to give you it raw and uncut. You know you can trust me. I never want to see you hurting because hurting you means hurting me and my son. So, I came over here to cook you breakfast and to listen to you."

"Look, I appreciate that shit, Carmen. I don't need to vent, but even if I did, I ain't the type of nigga to vent to my woman. My demons are just that, mine. I don't want to tell you about the ugly side of my life. I want you to have happiness and get all the best things life has to offer you. That's why a nigga decided to just fall back, so my shit doesn't fall on you. Real shit, Carmen, it was selfish of me to not want you to go to school. That's a good look. Do your shit and I'ma get my shit together. When I step to you next time, all my shit will be together. Deal?" He asked, stepping up to me and giving me a kiss.

"Deal." I smiled.

This wasn't the way I picture this conversation going, but I wasn't mad at it. Hopefully, Raulin meant what he said because I wanted my family. I'll take my time to focus on me and my son, but I wouldn't wait forever.

One Year Later

Chapter 29 Richboy

I smiled as I threw one-dollar bills on a stripper as they danced at Club Fashion in Detroit. After I hit the lick on Raul, I thought about staying in Columbus. However, after some serious thinking, I thought that it would be too hot. Detroit wasn't too far from the city and after laying low for a while these last few months, I been able to make major moves. I built me a crew and my name was ringing more bells than Christmas time in the city.

"Freak bitch!" I smacked the stripper who was giving me a lap dance on her ass as I looked over to my right-hand man, G-Baby.

"Aye, nigga, I'm about to head out. A nigga too lit," I said to G-baby, who I met when I first came to Detroit.

"Need me to roll with you?" G-baby asked.

"Hell nah, nigga, enjoy yourself. This our fucking city, ain't nobody gon' fuck with me!!" I said and G-baby chuckled before giving me dap.

I staggered out of the bar and hit the button on his key fob. I around and nobody was outside, the parking lot was quiet and dark. Heading over to where I parked my car . I chuckled as I thought about my life. I finally got a taste of being at the top. I was ecstatic to hear about Detective Robinson's demise and knew I would have his freedom. I was never questioned as a suspect in Diamond's murder. It was just another cold case in Columbus and I was happy about that. The only person who could actually tie me to the scene was Detective Robinson, and he was no longer amongst the living, so I wasn't worried. Nobody even knew I was snitching, but Rissa and she was gone. I still held respect in the streets of Columbus and although I no longer resigned there, that was a plus to me. Detroit wasn't too far from the city. The last thing I needed was for word to get back to Detroit that I was a rat. It would be detrimental to all the business ventures I had going on.

"I'm that motherfucking nigga!" I screamed out loud to no one in particular. The liquor mixed with my new fame and money had me feeling himself.

"Damn, I didn't think it would be yuko I'll this easy to catch your ass slipping." I heard the voice from behind me and didn't bother to turn around. I let out a breath and look around to see if anyone was in sight. I looked at my car parked a few feet away and thought about making a run for it. My gun was in the car because we weren't allowed to have them in Club Fashion. It didn't matter who it was, the club owner, Roscoe, didn't play that.

"How the fuck you find me?" I finally asked, turning around to face Raulin.

"You thought Detroit was a far away enough city for me. Nigga, my name known in states, including this one. You ready to die, nigga?" Raul asked, aiming his gun at my head. I wasn't sure if there were cameras, but the all black hoodie he had on did a lot to disguise Raul's true identity. *Damn!* I thought knowing this would be my last day on earth.

Chapter 30 Raul

I waited patiently for this moment. I played the back and let Richboy get comfortable. I had eyes on him from the moment he left the city. I watched as he built a whole new life in Detroit off the money I put my blood, sweat and grind into.

"Come on, Raul, don't do this shit, man," Richboy begged, looking at the gun then the empty duffel bags I was holding in his other hand.

"Nigga, stop begging, that's some hoe ass shit. Take me to your stash spot, nigga!" I barked and Richboy sat there. Hitting him with the gun, I shook my head as Richboy whimpered.

"Let's go, nigga!" I said again, and this time, Richboy complied. He unlocked his door and I slid in the driver seat, never taking my gun off him.

"Do some hoe shit and I'll kill you!" I told him and Richboy nodded his head. He knew the kind of person I was so, he wasn't taking no chances. As I drove, I could tell Rich Boy had a lot on his mind. I bet he was trying to figure out how he could get out of his current situation with his life still intact.

"Damn, nigga, my money got you living," I said when you we pulled up to the big gated home that was Richboy's . One million dollars. that's how much Richboy probably put down on the house. This shit was nice as fuck.

"Let's go, nigga!" I barked and Richboy opened the door. I followed behind him and got out of the car. Once inside the home, Richboy's eyes scanned the room. I bet He had guns hidden all over. His mind probably was racing as he thought of different plans to try and get to one.

Boom! Boom!

"Ahhhhh! Nigga, what the fuck was that for?!" Richboy screamed out in agonizing pain as he dropped to the floor. I had shot him in both legs. I came here to murder Richboy today, so the silencer was already on his gun.

"I ain't fucking around, nigga. Where that stash at?" I barked, pointing the gun at Richboy again.

"It's upstairs, second door to the right, under the floor board." I nodded my head, walked by Richboy, stopped, then turned back around. Heading over to where Richboy was, I beat him with my gun. Richboy cried out in

pain, but that did nothing to move me. Once I saw all the
blood pouring from Richboy's head, he stopped and headed
up stairs to the room where Richboy told him the money
was. Lifting up the floor boards, I came face to face with
blue bills stacked up neatly. Lifting up another part of the
floor, I saw the work. I thought hard and long about taking
that too. Instead, I took the duffle bags I had in his hand
and only collected the money. I wanted my family back
and I knew the only way to get them back was to
successfully bow out the game. It was hard for me seeing
Carmen and trying to control my feelings. Same as it was
for her. I didn't want to step to Carmen and history repeats
itself with the arguments we used to have about me being
in the streets. I wanted to be better for my son and
Carmen, I owed them that much.

After filling up the two duffle bags, I headed
downstairs to see Richboy shaking his head and on his
stomach, trying to crawl towards the doors. I chuckled then
shot him in the back of his head.

"Hoe ass nigga," I said as I stepped over his body
then walked out the door. I walked two miles before I
called for an Uber to take me back to the club where my
car was.

Still Caught Up With A Trap God

Chapter 31 Carmen

I walked into the backyard and smiled at the scene in front of me. Niomi, Renz, Rayven, Diggy, Jaliyah and her boyfriend all sat in the backyard at Renz and Niomi's home, drinking and laughing. The kids were off to the side in the play pen. I smiled as I thought about how big the kids had gotten, even my son.

"Congrats, best, I'm proud of you." I walked over to Jaliyah. She had graduated school and had her degree.

"You're up next," Jaliyah said, hugging me.

I had another year because of the break I took from school, but I knew that I would get a degree too. School has been going great for me. Elijuan tried to be friends still, but I ignored him. I told myself I wasn't waiting on Raul, and that I didn't have the time to date anyone. That's why when men asked me out, I declined. Truth is, deep down, I was waiting on Raul. He put his mark on my heart and even though I hates to admit it, I knew I would always belong to him. He was my first and only.

"Where's my god baby?" Jaliyah asked.

"Raul should be bringing him any moment."

"Speaking of Raul, how are things between y'all two?"

"It's copacetic. I wish he would just put this street nigga mentality away and get on the same kind of shit my brother and Diggy are on. Look at them legal businesses, family men. They're taking the necessary steps to make their women happy, and to make sure they're safe. Maybe I'm not worth the change. I love him , but I deserve so much more than to be a baller's girl. I want to be the wife to a man. I don't want to one day have to tell my son daddy's not coming home because he's in jail or worse, he's been killed."

"You're worth that shit though," Raul said, approaching us. He held our son in his hands as I smiled at him.

"Momma's baby, I missed you." I gave him a kiss on the cheek. It's been a week since I last seen Raul he said he was going out of town. When he got back in town the very next day, he picked up our son and had been keeping him every day since. He said needed his son as a reminder to why he was doing what he was doing; stepping out the game.

"Let me take my god baby while y'all talk." Jaliyah took him and headed back to the backyard.

I stared at Raul. I loved this man whole heartily.

"Hey, how you been?" I asked, not really knowing what else to say to him.

"Look, Carmen. I don't want you to ever feel like you ain't good enough when it comes to me. You and my damn son are the best thing that happened to me. I had to go sit down with Ma's crazy ass, but she really put shit in perspective for me. A good woman comes around once in a lifetime, and I'm not trying to miss out on mine because I couldn't step away from the streets that don't love me. I know I ain't always been the perfect nigga, but from this moment forward, I promise to be that for you. I promise to love and protect you, be a great father, and a great partner, everything you need."

Getting on his knees, he grabbed my hand, and stared in my eyes. Before he could ask the question, I screamed.

Still Caught Up With A Trap God

"Ahhhhhhhhh!!!"

Everyone came running and when they saw Raul on his knees in front of me with a ring, they cheered.

"So, what's good? You trying be stuck with a nigga for a lifetime?" He asked and the guys chuckled.

"Wow, so romantic," Niomi joked and everyone laughed as they waited for my answer.

"Yea, I'll be stuck for a lifetime," I said and everyone clapped.

Renz walked over to me, kissed me on the head and gave me his blessing. Renz and Raul talked amongst themselves and I learned Renz been gave him his blessing. I was just new to the news, I watch as Renz looked around at his family. All of us were happy, all the kids were straight, and life was good. Niomi had started school for journalism, Raven was now opening a daycare, and I was so close to being done with school. We all overcame so much in life and in our relationships. Still, they all found the way to say strong. The men have put us women through a lot, but we stayed loyal and waited for our man to grow.

We went from being Caught up In A Trap God to being wives of Grown Men.

THE END.

CPSIA information can be obtained
at www.ICGtesting.com
Printed in the USA
LVHW041508051120
670844LV00002B/393